LB

459.2

WITHDRAWN

# Carel Weight

## A Haunted Imagination

To
Carel in Affectionate Regard
and
in Memory of E.R.A. Sewter
Beloved Master of *Psellus*
and the *Comneni*

# A Haunted Imagination

**R. V. WEIGHT**

David & Charles

A DAVID & CHARLES BOOK

Copyright © text R.V. Weight 1994
Copyright © illustrations Carel Weight 1994
First published 1994

A catalogue record for this book is available from the British Library.

ISBN 0 7053 0183 7

Photograph on page 6 courtesy of Mike Fear.

Typeset by Ace Filmsetting Ltd, Frome, Somerset
and printed in Singapore by C.S. Graphics Ltd
for David & Charles
Brunel House  Newton Abbot  Devon

# ACKNOWLEDGEMENTS

I cannot sufficiently acknowledge the debt I owe to Professor Carel Weight, without whose unfailing encouragement and help this work could not have been undertaken. Patiently, and with immense generosity, he has furthered my work in every possible way.

To Miss Helen Roeder I owe a special debt of gratitude for allowing me access to Carel Weight's war-time correspondence, which provided the material for the artist's experience in the ranks. And I am grateful to Professor Eileen Hogan and the Camberwell Press for permission to make use of their publication *The Curious Captain*, Weight's letters to Miss Roeder during his service as Official War Artist in Europe.

I am particularly indebted to Mr John Hyams, who read the text and advised me on essential revisions, and to my friend Mrs Ida Dickie for listening to the material chapter-by-chapter as first drafted. I must thank Mr John Gardiner very warmly for his invaluable advice and Mr George Weight, the family genealogist, for affording me a vivid glimpse of the painter's early life.

My sincere thanks are due to Claudia Brigg who, as picture researcher, has been untiringly painstaking and efficient, and whose specialist skills have been indispensable.

I have every reason to be grateful to my editor, Alison Elks, for her support and forbearance and for having done so much to further the publication of this book.

I sincerely thank the many collectors and custodians for their help and allowing me access to their pictures. They include:

Arts Council of Great Britain; Bernard Jacobson Gallery; Bradford City Art Gallery; Royal Pavilion Art Gallery and Museum, Brighton; Royal West of England Academy, Bristol; British Library; Robin Bynoe; Herbert Art Gallery, Coventry; Peter Dakeyne; Desmond Austin and Phipps; Eggar Holdings Ltd; Fieldborne Galleries, London (Bernard Sternfield); Fine Art Society, London; New Metropole Arts Centre, Folkestone; Sir Brinsley Ford CBE, Hon. FRA, FSA; Alexander Patrick Greysteil Hore-Ruthven, 2nd Earl of Gowrie; Barnfield Museum, Halifax (Nigel Herring); Hastings Museum and Art Gallery; Mrs Desmond Heyward; Mr and Mrs Jeffrey Horwood; Mr and Mrs Hudson-Lyons; Imperial War Museum, London (Miss J. Wood and M. Moody); Inner London Education Authority; Leeds City Art Gallery (Alex Robertson); J.R.M. Keatley; Linda Kitson; Mr and Mrs David Knox; Walker Art Gallery, Liverpool (Alex Kitson); Longman Group UK (R. Fletcher, Mrs Kate Cawdell, Guy Hills); Dean and Canons of Manchester Cathedral; Manchester City Art Gallery; F. Manzi; F.A. Marwood; Mr and Mrs Alfred Mignano; Nottingham Castle Museum; Oldham Art Gallery (Mrs Tessa Gudgeon); Ashmoleon Museum, Oxford; Harris Museum and Art Gallery, Preston; Mrs Alys Rickett; Nicholas Rickett; Reading Museum and Art Gallery (Godfrey Omer-Parsons); Royal Academy of Arts, London (Miss E. Lindsay, Miss H. Valentine, N. Savage); St Paul's Church, Harefield (Revd C. Stanley); Saatchi Collection, London; Simon Langton Grammar School, Canterbury (Headmaster and Bursar); Somerset County Museum, Taunton; Sotheby's, London (Susan Kent); Tate Gallery, London; Helen Valentine (Royal Academy of Arts); Mrs Shirley Valentine; Dr and Mrs Andrew Verney; Dame Rebecca West; York City Art Gallery.

I should like to acknowledge most warmly the kind help from numerous other sources. They include the following individuals, libraries and publications:

*Apollo*; *The Artist*; *The Art Review*; Barrie & Jenkins (Professor Christopher Frayling); *The Burlington Magazine*; Brandler Galleries, Brentwood (John Brandler); Cambridge University Library (John Reynolds and staff of the Reading and West Rooms); Cambridge University Press (Dr Robin Kirkpatrick); Faber & Faber; Donald Hamilton-Fraser RA; Hereford City Library; *Hereford Times*; Hertfordshire College of Art and Design, St Albans; Hitchin Library, Hertfordshire; Mervyn Levy ARCA; *Modern Painters – A Quarterly Journal of the Fine Arts*; Mr and Mrs Nicholas Nodes; Oxford University Press; *The Painter and Sculptor*; R. G. Powell; Deirdre Redmond (Irish Ladies' Hockey Union, Dublin); Michael Rooney RA; Royal Academy of Arts, London (Information and magazine); *The Studio*; *Times* Newspapers Ltd; Weidenfeld & Nicolson; Westminster City Art Library.

# CONTENTS

---

The artist, Carel Weight.

6 August 1992

Dear Ray

I have just read your manuscript of the book and I want to tell you that I think it is the first piece of art criticism that I have read since Lord Clark, which is a work of art in itself. It is written with such simplicity that a child could understand and I feel very proud that my pictures could inspire it. It is completely different to so much criticism we are used to, that is incomprehensible. It comes from the heart.

I thought you might like to have my feelings on it.

Yours


Sunday

Dear Ray

When I went out this morning to post my letter to you I was far from happy with it and when I reached the pillarbox I had an idea and I scribbled on the envelope that it might be called something like – 'A guide to the paintings of Carel Weight'. That started me thinking. I always felt that it was the most original book about a painter I had ever come across. It was an investigation derived entirely by looking at the pictures with infinite care and sympathy and reading my intentions which I could hardly have believed possible. It was closer to poetry than the ordinary art history, Freudism and all the other isms. But how much more readable and exciting.

I just thought I would send this extra scribble.

Yours

# PREFACE

A common interest in Stanley Spencer – my signature closely followed Carel's in the first Visitors' Book in the Cookham Gallery – led, many years later, to my meeting Carel Weight and to his generous help with this monograph. He has introduced me to collectors and friends who, in their turn, have welcomed me and indulged my cluttering their rooms with photographic paraphernalia. I have been given free access to their private collections, and been privileged to photograph early paintings, few of which have been on public exhibition. I am deeply indebted to them for their encouragement and for their discerning comments which have proved indispensable in clarifying interpretation.

Carel Weight's instruction was that I should deal with his pictures and not himself. I have respected his wish, I hope, without concealing too much of his endearing warmth and kindness and marvellous sense of fun. Work on this monograph has been most enjoyable. It is impossible to acknowledge adequately my indebtedness to him. For some time I have felt there was a need for a monograph on Carel Weight which would concentrate on his craftsmanship, the dynamics of his work and the unique quality of his poetry. I hope what I have done may go some way towards supplying the need.

R.V.W

**Rose (1929)**
*Oil on panel, 9 × 7in (22.8 × 17.7cm),*
*artist's collection.*

# 1

## AFFINITIES, AVERSIONS AND ART
## Narrative and Visionary

---●---

He recalls a sympathetic teacher who 'Whenever there was a quiet time, would say: "Come along, and tell the class one of your stories." I seem to have had little difficulty in weaving some romance. Something would surface which seemed quite popular. I was about seven, and not very shy at that age.'

And at that age the romances were of fairy marvels, not of ghosts and night-terrors.

Carel Weight is a born storyteller. We wonder what will happen next, what's round the corner, what his wraith-like, surging trees and ominous skies portend. The narrative potential is present in portraiture, while townscape and landscape are, more often than not, stages for the traffic of his drama.

None the less, Carel Weight's first concern is with design, pattern, composition and, above all, with the function of colour.

> My pictures are primarily a relationship of figures to a setting. The narrative aspect of
> my painting is something that comes later, and in a way of its own accord.[1]

The shock following that first happy experience of school was extreme and has haunted him ever since – the harsh regime of a vicious-minded, tyrannical headmaster. And there was a terrifying grandfather, ruthless and evil-natured.

Early childhood was lonely and unsettled. His parents, who worked long, strenuous hours – his mother had additional social commitments – entrusted him to Rose, a widowed acquaintance who lived with her old mother in Chelsea. They were poor, lovable women whose devotion Carel returned with interest. He adored them, 'more even I suppose than my own parents'.[2] Later, this circumstance led him to reflect on the ambiguous rather than the redemptive nature of love. But the redemptive is acknowledged where that is due – in, for instance, *Captain Kitson and his Granddaughter, Linda* (1978, page 99), and in the portrait of *Rose* (1929, page 8), who mothered him and was in every respect his foster mother, save only in law.

Carel was about four when they moved from the small Chelsea home to a flat in Dawes Road, Fulham. It was above a shoe shop, No 184, and was certainly cheaper, but very tiny. Carel and Henry, Rose's son, shared the boxroom, but their interests lay far apart.

Henry was Carel's senior by ten years – 'He was very superior to me, and could think of nothing else but engines and motor cars' – interests which were of little appeal to the unmechanically minded Carel. So Henry was neither soulmate nor playmate – relationships beneath the dignity of his advanced years. His later ambition was to play in a jazz band; he practised his banjo remorselessly, and the box-cum-bedroom reverberated in dreadful amplification. Such conditions did not further Carel's progress at school, but he lived there until he entered the Hammersmith School of Art in about 1926. He spent the weekends in the comparative luxury of his parents' home – their comfortable flat in Paddington – so that, from the first, very different conditions contributed to the forming of his responses. 'The contrast was crucial . . . My playgrounds were the broken-down streets, alleys and parks of South West London.'[3]

Carel was born on 10 September 1908 in the Borough of Paddington, and received his early education firstly at the Sherbrook Road Board School, an Infants' School for children of the less well-off, and later at Sloane Secondary School, Chelsea, 'a rough secondary school where I was a very bad pupil'[4] – which, in the circumstances just outlined, is not surprising.

He confesses that 'It was all rather uncomfortable. My father did all he could to persuade me to return home. But no – I preferred to stay put—'

I interrupted.

*Self*: 'Was that because of Rose's personality, so very warm, and—?'
*Carel* (interrupting also): 'It was not only that. I was not being told off and corrected all the time as my parents

**The Musicians (1932)**
*Oil on panel, 32 × 60in (81.2 × 152.4cm),*
*Guy Hills for Longman Group UK.*

would have done. . . I wasn't rebellious in the least – the very reverse, in fact. I accepted everything they said, and myself said very little. Then, too, I'd made my friends. There was the butcher's son next door, and opposite a Jewish family I was particularly fond of. And I was free to move about, and mix with all kinds of people – some of them very odd – and I got a lot out of these early friendships. Had I gone back to my parents I'd have been very lonely. They'd have been out a great deal, and continually telling me that I was using cockney words, that I should mind my Ps and Qs – all that sort of thing. As I got older they became less unbearable. My mother usually found something we could talk about. My father felt I'd be very unworthy of him – that he'd have to keep me even in his years of retirement.'

Carel's father, Sidney Weight, spent his life as a cashier in a city bank at work he loathed, all the time longing for an open-air life. The outbreak of World War I was a melancholy fulfilment of the wish. He served in the Artists' Rifles, and was later commissioned in the Royal Artillery. 'I inherited what talent I have from my father. . . He had an artist inside wanting to get free. It never did. It was imprisoned for life in a grim office in the City from 9 to 6.'[5]

Weight remembers some two or three drawings made by his father during his service in the Artillery: 'Officers were trained to make accurate drawings of terrain, enemy positions and so on.' Poor Sidney Weight. It was scarcely an excursion into art. But his son's achievement was a source of pride, 'And he'd warned me about "starving in a garret", but anything I did which pleased him he'd carry off to the City to show his friends in the bank.'

After his mother's death, Carel Weight searched the house from top to bottom for his father's drawings, but without success. 'They'd vanished totally. And I'd have cherished them more than a priceless Old Master.' 'He was always a very unhappy man,' he told Mervyn Levy. 'His commissioned rank around the level of Lieutenant, as I remember it . . . was the pinnacle of his success.'[6]

Carel's mother, Blanche Harriet, though born in England, was of mixed German and Swedish blood. Her father, whose name was Süssenbach, came from Hamburg and, on settling in England, changed the family

**The Dogs (1955–56)**
*Oil on board, 48 × 96in (121.9 × 243.8cm), Tate Gallery, London.*

name to Williams. He was an extremely gifted chiropodist whose clients included such stars as Fritz Kreisler and Enrico Caruso; most famous of all was the King, Edward VII. Weight's mother was also a chiropodist, having been trained by her father. A manicurist, too, she 'specialised in attending to the hands and feet of the acting profession'.[7] Hers was a warm, winning personality, sharing a passion for music with her sad, dispirited husband. She encouraged him to stand up to his bullying father – which he did, and was promptly cut out of his father's will. Such was Louis Petit Weight: the ogre-grandfather of Carel's childhood. He was 'a really terrible man. He was a bully and . . . was cruel to his wife and children. He had a wine and spirits shop and was successful in retiring from business at a comparatively early age. My father had no love for his relatives and never talked about them. He always said my mother rescued him from them.'[8]

Rose was an excellent foster mother. Not particularly well educated, she was, however, well read and her shelves were stocked with a supply of good books, including the works of Shakespeare. She knew many of the Shakespeare plots, which she would recount to Carel, and at night would read to him such popular fiction as Baroness Orczy's *Scarlet Pimpernel* and *She* by Rider Haggard. He vividly remembers her introducing him to Roget's *Thesaurus* – a testimony to the ingenuity of her teaching skill. Dickens was also part of her curriculum. He came to Ainsworth later. 'She was also psychic – she could predict things with uncanny accuracy.'[9]

Carel Weight tells us he was bad at school. But he was blessed with the creative gift, and any sense of failure was offset by his imaginative life, which London stimulated, even as it provoked the images of Blake's visions. But for both, war darkened the beloved city.

There is a magnificent design, *Jerusalem 26*, which Blake inscribed:

> *Such visions have appear'd to me*
> *As I my order'd race have run.*

It is a vision of evil passion and error. Flames surround a gigantic figure and the Serpent of Error coils about his shoulders. Could such visions have appeared to Weight?

Silent presences hovered in the night sky – Zeppelins which woke the batteries to frenzied reaction. By day the hospitalised appeared on the streets, shell shocked, hobbling between crutches, ashen and flushed with phthisis, the image of the face of war.

Other images haunted Weight's childhood. Not angels rustling their wings in Peckham Rye – more likely the Medusa's head hissing with the swish of the headmaster's cane.

The symbolism of the snakes, still vigorously writhing, keeps alive the buried horror of these two awful people.[10]

And he tells us that his grandfather has stayed in his mind as 'an emblem of sheer fear'.

Carel Weight's symbolism – unlike Blake's, which reinforces didacticism – clarifies meaning, is marvellously productive of atmosphere and stimulates response. He is all for 'audience participation', but on the whole this is more for fullness of reaction than for any instructive purpose.

Duly, there appeared other, more generous images. Barnes Station, the Albert Bridge, Bishop's Park, a drab corner in a sleazy suburb were to impress upon him their visionary potential.

Wordsworth's reaction to the massacres of the Terror was compounded of 'remembrances and dim admonishments' known earlier in solitude and desolation. Weight confesses that for the lonely child to live in his imagination, particularly under the conditions just outlined, 'is to live with fears and terrors'. It is easy to envisage the solitary, only child under such imaginative pressures that, as with Wordsworth, they became external presences. 'Remembrances' of the fearful grandfather, 'dim admonishments' from the dreadful headmaster, the cries of 'doomed youth', would have moved the child deeply and have led, much later, to the extreme showings of his apocalypse.

In his article 'The Way I Work' in *Painter and Sculptor*, Weight wrote:

> The products of memory, mood and imagination rise upon a foundation of fact. My art is concerned with such things as anger, love, hate, fear and loneliness emphasised by the setting in which the drama is played.
>
> Perhaps there is something Wordsworthian in all this, but fundamentally I feel that it has its roots in my earliest childhood.[11]

**The Speed Merchant (1956)**
*Oil on panel, 24 × 36in (60.9 × 91.4cm),*
*David Knox collection.*

**Dangerous Corner (c.1956)**
*Oil on canvas, 38 × 48in (96.5 × 121.9cm),*
*private collection.*

Weight's is a haunted poetry – violent, fantastic and macabre. That is the essence of his most characteristic work. But such a summary overlooks the contemplative subject and ignores its strains of compassion and humour. Tensions that stem from environment and circumstance beget the poetry creative of much we find uncomfortable in his work. Such tensions were to be treated later in the course of his 'swelling scene'.

But it is best to begin at the beginning with *The Musicians* (1932, page 10), initially entitled *The Enraged Musician*. It is a good starting point, being, in several respects, autobiographical and the first picture Weight painted at Goldsmith's. He had moved there in 1929 to escape the rigidity of his earlier training at Hammersmith where 'no one taught composition, and no one showed any concern for the emotional aspects of painting'.[12] Here at Goldsmith's, he could paint the sort of pictures he wanted to.

Reading from the left, we see, looking from an upper window, Cézanne – one of Carel Weight's early heroes. Below, a group is being interrupted by a tall, bowing figure, based on Weight himself, offering his hat for their supportive pence. In the centre, two lanky street musicians – one of them also a version of the painter – pull and push on their noisy accordions. A dwarf trombone player, modelled on a fellow student, blows zealously somewhere in the region of the accordion players' knees. It is all too much for the professional musician seen on the far right in the tiny window of his Academy of Music. This personage – tucked away from the action in the manner of Bruegel – was Carel Weight's painting master, James Bateman, afterwards an RA. On this side another group is assembled, their interest divided between the musicians and their own imperious need for a good gossip. In the group is a tall, handsome woman in a white blouse and flowered skirt. In the letter[13] written to the present owner of the picture (the full text is given in the Notes), he explained that this lady was his foster mother. The lady opposite, wearing the large 'cockney hat', was his mother.

The scene is buoyantly coloured, the groups gaily dressed – an exuberant, carefree episode, conceived and executed *con brio*, heightened by the broad humour of the enraged professional. As far as those out of doors are concerned – prominent in their finery or display of quasi-musical expertise – the maestro can stay aerated.

It was, as Weight wrote in his letter, 'probably the most personal picture I ever painted'. It has about it a primitive freshness which reminds me of Chagall's early work. And I find – I hope not perversely – a similar reference in *An Episode in the Childhood of a Genius* (1932). Weight did admit to 'several elements having gone

**George Cruikshank: Jack Sheppard Escaping from Clerkenwell Prison (1839)** *Steel engraving, from the novel* **Jack Sheppard** *by W.H. Ainsworth. By permission of the British Library.*

into its making'. It is the second of a group of four such early pictures, and will be considered in the next chapter.

Disquiet in the suburbs is only part of the staple of the world of Carel Weight. One critic immoderately declared that *The Presence* (1955, page 110) 'is so quintessentially Carel Weight that, in seeing through it, one seems to see into all his work'.[14] I began with *The Musicians* partly to counter a summary judgment of that sort. Other paintings, too numerous to mention, could also oppose so extravagant an assertion.

At times, Weight's work reflects directly the scene which prevailed around him. *Clapham Junction* (1978) is a good example, in which two policemen chase a gang of young roughs who are up to no good. And despite my jolly start with *The Musicians*, there can be no denying that, like Charles Dickens who preferred night as his time for walking, Weight, too, is addicted to shadowy gothic obscurities, and the more extreme the better.

> I feel less inspired by sunshine. . . I get stimulated walking at twilight, perhaps seeing
> things taking on extraordinary shapes, and that kindles one's imagination.[15]

The straitened purlieus of broken-down streets and alleys, the suburban playground he knew as a child, suggested uneasy goings-on, even as M.R. James found places productive of his ghosts. Besides personal experience, other elements from Hogarth, Cruikshank and 'Phiz', Ensor and Munch helped furnish out Carel Weight's skeleton cupboard of effects. There was also Rose's capacity for the occult which gave a head start to his development as a visionary. He tells us that

> in one of my Crucifixions a great claw-like hand gradually materialised as if the whole
> composition were held in its safe, omnipotent grasp.[16]

Thus – and we are approaching the psychological process Wordsworth describes in the famous episode referred to above – the environment could appear

> unfit for the repose of night,
> Defenceless as a wood where tigers roam.[17]

There is, in fact, one instance where the haunting evidently breaks through the imaginative confines, so that

> There is a likelihood that the 'Presence' is not just a figment of my own imagination.
> Someone . . . got in touch with me and said that this was the time of day (the dusk)
> when she herself had seen the apparition.[18]

He spoke to me further about this, saying that his correspondent had 'seen the ghost many times in exactly the same place I'd shown it in the picture. . . I don't know what all that means. I just included it to add to the interest of the picture.' The scene of this painting, *The Presence* (1955, page 110), is Bishop's Park, Fulham, an unlikely enough place to attract communications from the 'other side of silence'.

The narrative artist faces the perennial pitfall of slipping into illustration and, although the Pre-Raphaelites failed in this, their attempts to create the archaic or ideal resulted in a world of strained effects – tense, theatrical and dream-like. It shares something with the world of Carel Weight, though this is one which concentrates more on the telling relationship between subject and setting. 'I aim to create a world superficially close to the visual one but a world of greater tension and drama.'[19] This superficial closeness is the essence of Carel Weight's world. In *The Dogs* (page 11) a strange force activates the scene. Vehicles awkwardly negotiate the crowded area. Two cyclists belt, hell for leather, across the foreground as if to contest priorities with the emerging taxi. A man strolls along as if in a world of his own, unaware of the taxi pressing forward immediately behind him.

The thrills of the evening fade slowly. The crowd awakens to individual worlds of responsibility and care. The sun, fumed over by an industrial haze, goes down on a scene – familiar yet oddly out of joint.

Nor is this world confined to the London suburbs. There are rural settings, 'tensed-up' by odd relationships – juxtapositions sometimes quite innocent, and often humorous. *The Village Cup Tie* (1947) is a good example. Be it rural or urban, it is a world of emanations, of much natural beauty, troubled – almost always – by an

H.K. Browne, 'Phiz'. The Conjurors
Interrupted (1855)
*Steel engraving, from the novel* **Mervyn
Clitheroe** *by W.H. Ainsworth. By
permission of the British Library.*

unexpected element. In his most recent work it has become outré and nightmarish.

In *Crucifixion* of 1959 (page 51), already mentioned, the fusion of vision and craftsmanship was such that Weight had to submit to spiritual dictates

> when . . . the great rock on which the Cross was standing had mysteriously taken the
> shape of a hand although I had no such idea in my mind while I was working.[20]

Try as he would to reshape the rock, it reasserted its form insistently and he was obliged to let it be – a Blakean process if ever there was one.

> I like what Dickens said that he created his characters and they ran away with him, and
> that's what happens with me and my pictures.[21]

That is when Weight is at his best, but there are times when the visionary power fails and little more results than superior illustration. I would instance *The Speed Merchant* (1956, page 12). In this we see at once the vital relationship between the movement of the cyclist, the curves and counter-curves of palings and wall, the swirling yellow sky, the conifers bending and whipping in the strong, following wind. But such cohesive principles are present in the best of Cruikshank and 'Phiz'. Both, however, lack Carel Weight's understanding of colour. Of such a work, Grey Gowrie wrote:

> The atmosphere, it seems to me, is literary in the contrived and artificial sense, the
> experience behind the painting is unauthentic.[22]

Compare another picture, *Dangerous Corner* (c.1956, page 13), which is equally 'on the move' but altogether more humanly aware. Involved as we are with these everyday risks – and maybe concerned on more than one account – we are interested parties in the fate of the little dog and are anxious for what is to happen next.

It is, relatively, a moment of quiet anxiety. A lorry rounds the corner too quickly – it slumps down on its springs. Directly in its path, a spaniel crossing the road is urged to hurry to heel. And perhaps the lad, dismounting from his cycle for safety's sake and carried along by his own momentum, is stopping to talk to the girl whose head and shoulders enter the foreground as she starts to cross. Only allow the fancy its rein and we could feel ourselves in rivalry with him for her attention! And yet the trees could suggest a serious outcome, gaunt, dark and wintry, sinister and powerfully articulate.

Quite complex reactions, easily provoked by the compulsive spell of Carel Weight at his best. *The Speed Merchant* is of too single an interest to stimulate anything like such a varied reaction.

We may envisage the boy who was 'bad at school, good at art' so beguiled by the illustrations that he ventures into the world of Dickens. He was a great admirer of those drawings, he told me. 'In fact, one can't think of Dickens without the illustrations.' He had read Ainsworth, as we know, most likely in those editions to which Cruikshank and 'Phiz' had contributed their finest work. Those novels – amalgams of the gothic and historical – required the 'glooms', the brooding atmosphere, the animism and dash Weight elevates to the status of art. Cruikshank's billowing and striated sky under which Jack Sheppard escapes from Clerkenwell Prison (page 14), the alarming shapes taken by 'Phiz's' trees in the sinister gloaming (page 15), find echoes in Weight's *The Evening Stroll* and *The Watcher* (1991, opposite).

Hammersmith College of Art insisted on the prime importance of drawing from life:

> If figures appeared in a painting, it was vital that they should be correct anatomically –
> never distorted to express an emotional state. I was at loggerheads with that. If I asked
> how I should paint an imaginary subject, I was told: 'Find a tree, or something – build
> up your picture, then work in some of your life drawings to give it a basis of reality.'. . .
> I found it didn't work. I couldn't get a model to adopt a position which I felt at all
> significant.

As for engraving, whatever views Weight may have held they were not furthered by the dry, formal manner in which the subject was presented. 'The British engravers were marvellous,' he said. Then, looking beyond Blake, 'Until a blight set in with their attempts to over-perfect results too consciously.' A lifeless presentation of such an enclosed speciality was tedious in the extreme to one who, for some time, had been anxious to strike out on his own. But Blake was the exception whom he admired 'enormously', so that we cannot overlook the famous dictum:

> The great and golden rule of art . . . is this – that the more distinct, sharp, and wiry the
> bounding line, the more perfect the work of art.[23]

In much of Weight's art, Blake's 'hard and wiry' line achieves its aim of 'rectitude and certainty'. Perhaps it was with those demands in mind that he told Norman Rosenthal, Director of Exhibitions in the Royal Academy, that when he painted a portrait he 'drew with great precision'.

We may see this 'bounding line' well exemplified in the first portrait of *Orovida Pissarro* (1956, page 57). The *Portrait of an Actor-Poet* (1979, page 97) provides an even better example, and there are further instances too numerous to mention.

Carel Weight would have scrutinised the etched line of Hogarth, Cruikshank and 'Phiz', and his admiration for the Pre-Raphaelites would have commended not only their strong colours, but their sheer definitions, too. Even were it possible to list every such influence, we would be left finally with his own unique management of line, in which he is wholly on his own. Nowhere is that more clearly demonstrated than when line brings into focus his beloved suburban world – in the architecturally drawn villas, the streets, walls and gardens, above all in the convoluted pattern of branches against a blazing sunset. Of this last feature *The Presence* (1955, page 110) is the finest example.

Some four years after the first showing of *The Presence*, a reviewer complained of 'the lack of drawing of figures and of tree-anatomy'.[24] The figures in *The Musicians* answer the first complaint. As for the second, I suspect the critic is at odds with the artist's purpose, and that he would prefer trees to be closer to botanical exactitude than vital entities of dramatic poetry.

**The Watcher (1991)**
*Oil on board, 23½ × 11⅜in (59.5 × 29cm),*
*Robin Bynoe collection.*

# 2

# PORTRAITS
# A CHANGE IN DIRECTION
## Still-Life and Early Masterpieces in Portraiture and Landscape

———————————————— • ————————————————

Carel Weight seeks the place for his visionary showings and responds to its spirit as immediately as Stanley Spencer. The mood of a place affects the figures, influences their relationships and itself reflects their tensions. On the other hand, it may offset human disquiet within a peaceful garden, or against a calm, spacious landscape.

'My pictures always have to do with movement.' Of course, Weight was thinking of his familiar, violently active figures in their static settings. But, more significantly, the statement concerns the 'moving spirit', the poetic heart of a subject. We may illustrate the point by looking at two comparable pictures, *The Thames, Chiswick* 1938 (page 28) and *Teddington Lock* (1950, opposite). In the first, this 'moving spirit' is, paradoxically, in the suspense of autumn; in the second, it is in the ebullient surge of spring. The Chiswick painting uses discreetly modulated colours to evoke the softness and bright chill of early autumn. In the second, we sense that harshness, that certain 'left-over' from winter. A heavy downswing of grey cloud is flushed by a watery, unseen sun. At Chiswick, opposing forces are in balance, as the great body of water is checked under the weight of the incoming tide. At Teddington, a pleasure steamer makes for the lock, thrusting the river ahead of its prow in a rush of foam. Spectators, dressed sensibly in deference to the season, lean on the towpath rail or, from farther back, observe the river's animation. At Chiswick the lassitude of autumn is in the play of thin shadows on the road where two have stopped, a man and a woman, in desultory chat.

Seeing 'into the life of things',[1] Weight brings out that life subtly in one, vigorously in the other. Man and nature interrelate creatively to give reality to this 'moving spirit' in both works.

Carel Weight regards representation as an enjoyable challenge. More easily, more willingly than Stanley Spencer he detaches himself from his visionary forms and submits to the demands of even a commissioned portrait. 'I like portraiture for the same reason I like still life – for the discipline both departments impose, and I'm interested in people and like tracing the humanity in the study of a head.' Later, he would use certain devices to promote a kind of spiritual 'gearing-up', such as accessories and backgrounds to direct and deepen his responses. An insecure subject, for instance, might be shown against tilting furniture; or the floor may slope and give peremptoriness to the presentation; or the sitter's character may be indicated by a picture or two in the background. For example, *The World We Live In* (1970–73, page 89), whose subject is the breakdown of human relations in modern society, is sited behind the poor, failed *Actor-Poet* (1979). But these were later devices. For the present, the 'atmosphere' of personality is sufficient.

There are fine early portraits, carefully posed, carefully poised, in which precision of line is juxtaposed with a looser, swifter stroke. The portrait of *Rose* (1929, page 8) is in softer style – a bold head filling the panel, it might be indebted to Munch's many large heads of the *Sick Child* (1855–56). The bone structure is gently modelled, as befits the generous character with its concerned, tender expression.

Another mode is adopted for *The Red Gloves* (1932, page 20) painted three years later. The profile of a seated child is sharply defined in the strong light entering from the left. Then experimentation occurs with slashing strokes and a chunky, almost slapdash working of the gloves. 'It's quite a sombre picture,' Weight told me, 'with a strong light coming in from the left laying great emphasis on the brilliant red gloves. I painted it in one go, which wasn't bad for a young painter.'

He continued with a touchingly human sequel.

> My mother had noticed the child – a local fishmonger's daughter who was charmingly
> mannered and pretty. She would be an ideal subject for a portrait. If only she could be
> persuaded to sit, because she was terribly shy. So mother bribed her lavishly with

sweets, and on a rather cold day the little girl came to the studio wearing these thick, woollen, red gloves. I persuaded her to keep them on. Then – perhaps a bit too sternly – I told her that she must keep absolutely still, not a flicker of an eyelid. I rewarded her with a bottle of her favourite sweets, but – much to my surprise – she didn't seem as overjoyed as I'd hoped. She seemed more worried, if anything. I was quite mystified.

Until, that is, he returned to the studio, where a tiny pool beneath the chair betrayed the cause of the little girl's concern. He went on:

I took my mother to task. I told her that, in future, I would view with suspicion any model she might recommend.

And it is possible that, after this, he would think twice before completing another portrait 'in one go' – an achievement he'd spoken of with obvious pride. The child, proud, diffident all the same in her red gloves, emerges from the shadowy room with the strong light at her back in deference to her shyness. The picture was shown in his first one-man exhibition in 1933 in the Cooling Galleries.

Carel Weight was now twenty-four. He had spent three years at Hammersmith College of Art, and then for the past three years had studied part-time at Goldsmith's College. In both places the chief discipline was figure drawing, but Goldsmith's, as we have seen, encouraged him to make departures of his own choosing.

Of course there were good teachers at Hammersmith. I respected James Bateman in particular. He was in sympathy with my ambitions, and when he left for a better post at Goldsmith's, I followed. . . Goldsmith's was passing through a very interesting part of its history. Graham Sutherland was a student, though I never got to know him very well.

But Goldsmith's gave full rein to his imagination, and *The Musicians* was the first realisation of what he could accomplish, once allowed his head – something original and diverting, and a striking arrangement of figures in a setting.

Goldsmith's not only furthered his originality, it also introduced him to Helen Roeder, a fellow-student whose sensibilities were a counterpart of his own and with whom he established a lifelong companionship.

A few of his letters to Helen survive from the 1930s. He tells her (1935) of a hair-raising tour of the West

**Teddington Lock (1950)**
*Oil on canvas, 18 × 30in (45.7 × 76.2cm),*
*Bernard Sternfield,*
*Fieldborne Galleries.*

**Allegro Strepitoso (1932)**
*Oil on panel, 27½ × 36in (69.8 × 91.4cm),*
*Tate Gallery, London / Sotheby's, London.*

Country with Ivor Williams, the Welsh painter, whose ramshackle car is unequal to Porlock Hill. The weather is dreadful. In reversing, Williams backs into a pile of stones and ruptures the petrol tank. Like the famous Dutch boy, Weight springs into the breach and plugs it with his finger. Despite the weather, he paints 'two little Vlaminckish studies' – stormy, atmospheric studies in a turbulent Fauvist style.

He reports earlier on *Allegro Strepitoso* (1932, above) that it is 'progressing slowly,' and that he has invented a lion which he is sure would 'make Lizzy jump' (Lizzy was Helen's close friend). He has also painted a portrait of his Uncle (Percy) 'in two hours which is really "the goods"!'

His taste in music is catholic. On a painting holiday at Winson Manor near Cirencester, he finds a 'wonderful assortment of gramophone records from *Little Mr* (sic) *Echo* to Mahler's *Song of the Earth*. In an early letter he tells Miss Roeder that he is 'going to Queen's Hall to a BBC concert: Handel, Bach, Ireland and Walton. Sounds wonderful!'

At this time his mother told him a story of vital importance to his development as an artist. As a little girl, she had clambered out of an upstair window, and made her precarious way along a narrow, projecting ledge to a neighbour's windowsill, tempted there by the bright blooms in the window-box. 'People in the street saw her and were terribly worried about her falling, but somehow they got her back.'

It introduced another line – humorous fantasy – and he developed it with gusto. It was to become a constant in so many purlieus of Carel Weight's world.

> That gave me an idea for a picture. I moved the scene to the outside of a pub, and
> substituted a young lad who'd climbed up the inn sign and perched himself precariously
> on top. He was causing great consternation not only to people in the pub but also
> among the crowd who'd gathered outside.

He dignified this with the title *An Episode in the Childhood of a Genius* (1932).

There is something Hogarthian about the agitated action in progress against the solid façade of the pub, whose long facia loudly proclaims the patronage of Messrs Watneys. To the right of the pub runs a road, wide and straight, to the farthest background. A clumsy-footed fellow crosses the road to join the excited assembly.

**(Opposite)**
**The Red Gloves (1932)**
*Oil on canvas, 25 × 18in (63.5 × 45.7cm),*
*The Garden House School.*

Their interest centres on a man clambering up a ladder to rescue the boy. This late arrival, striding so heavily across the road, is possibly a reference to the Sweeper in Chagall's *Dead Man* (1908), though quite without the ponderous subtleties of that figure.

Meantime, the boy's position atop the sign has become increasingly insecure. His movements cause the heavy board to swing in its frame, threatening imminent dislodgment.

The next was *Allegro Strepitoso* (page 21), also of this year. In this, leonine ferocity becomes a cuddly, pantomime docility, and the giraffes, with the air of gossips rather too superior to be anything but above all this nonsense, are smugly conscious of their eminent viewing points. The lady in red – actually the painter's mother – defends herself against the lion with her umbrella and the urgency she would bring to swatting a wasp.

As for the composition – it may be seen at once how skilfully the event is related to the setting. The lion's playful pounce upon the lady is reinforced by the swept-over tree, whose leafage corresponds to his heavy mane and outsize head. Between his cage, whose doors have swung open, and the giraffes' enclosure the space is alive with the vigorous fun of knockabout farce. The lady stands her ground – her red, brandished umbrella taking our attention to a second lady, also in red, straining as if against a strong wind to take to her heels in all the frenzy of mock panic. The uniformed maid – her cap is red-laced – begins a cumbersome flight, directed by the curve of the giraffes' enclosure. Two of these lofty animals regard the goings-on with interest. Another, dignified, stretches a yearning neck heavenwards and, with closing eyes, dismisses the episode as the foolery of human beings. A fourth peers at us with a direct, cool and assessing look. In the background, on their terrace monkeys are either getting on with their own diversions or are discussing the way the human show is likely to resolve.

It is a bravura performance in the best tradition of pantomime.

> I wanted it to be a humorous picture, and the lion to be a lovable lion. It was immediately successful. I showed it at some gallery and the Selection Committee clapped it.
> That was rather nice. I followed it with *The Amazing Aeronaut*.

This delightful naïvety (1933, right) – worthy of Douanier Rousseau himself – recalls Carel's childhood fear of the rackety primitive aero-engine.

'*The Amazing Aeronaut* is almost surreal,' said Norman Rosenthal in 1981,[2] nearly fifty years after its painting. But why the qualifying 'almost'? For we have the de-orienting images of the fevered dream, generative of the irrationale of the surreal. In the gap between two corner shops floats the Amazing Aeronaut, top-hatted, dressed with impeccable formality and contending with gravity in a flying bedstead. Weight tells us:

> It started as a dream. . . I must have got a touch of the sun, and had to go to bed in a darkened room. I fell into a deep, strange sleep.[3]

Into the dream there entered sounds from external reality: the racket of a primitive aero-engine and hoofs beating along the road.

> I went to the window and looked out. A terrified donkey was flying hell for leather down the street. Then I saw why! An aeroplane – an early type, about 1905, I suppose – was flying very low, between the houses.[4]

The picture has about it the aura of a waking dream in a child's semi-conscious mind, fevered, in this instance, and exaggerating.

They make an exuberant foursome, these early 'departures': *The Musicians* (1931), *An Episode in the Childhood of a Genius* and *Allegro Strepitoso*, both of 1932, and *The Amazing Aeronaut* of the following year.

Carel Weight had struck the vein of humorous fantasy all right. A year or two later it was richly exploited in his *Balloon Trip to the Moon* (c. 1933, page 25). It was, he told me, based on a very early film which burlesqued the idea.

He gives to it all the spirit of those seaside outings we enjoyed long ago – when we could only succumb to the pressure of every promotion paraded, such as Mr Batty's *WONDERFUL WINKLES* and his *WONDERFUL TRIP* to the toylike asymmetrical crescent which hangs in the sky of crimson-lake. A balloon begins its wobbling ascent into the extravaganza of colour, with a crackpot astronomer astride the top peering through his telescope at the terrestrial horizon and, presumably because of that, scratching his head. The margins are decorated with arabesques of kite strings and fish nets, masks and funny dolls with funny feet, fishes and so on.

Weight is drawing on material endeared to his childhood – from the delightful old comics: *Chips*, *The Monster*, *Comic Cuts* and the like (he confesses to having favoured *The Gem* and *The Magnet*). His *Balloon Trip to the Moon* echoes the twopenny-coloureds rather than the penny-dreadfuls. But for me, the *Balloon Trip* resembles more a plate from the *Songs of Innocence – Holy Thursday*, for instance, especially in its lower marginal decoration.

Now, to be very serious with a tribute from Bernard Jacobson in the catalogue of his exhibition in celebration of Weight's eightieth birthday:

> It's probably very embarrassing for him if I refer to Carel Weight as a saint, but that is what he seems to me, at least within the art world. Of course there have been many saints before this one – but this one paints like the devil!

**The Amazing Aeronaut, or Sun, Steam and Speed (1933)**
*Oil on panel, 25 × 22in (63.5 × 55.8cm), private collection / Sotheby's, London.*

In the *Balloon Trip to the Moon*, in all its ingenuous farce, there is the capacity to see as a little child with eyes of born-again innocence – the quality of both the seer and the saint. But, 'Something too much of this,' Carel Weight would say, unspeakably embarrassed.

He could turn from fantasies and submit without constraint to the discipline of the still life, such as *Dream about a Flower* (1933, page 26). There was no case of submitting to set courses, once his 'departures' were confirmed. 'I just paint straight on,' he said, dismissing with a smile my raising the question of 'turning points' – the implication being that he painted as he chose, and submitted only to the subject's demands.

There were no constraints, and during this early fanciful spell he painted numerous flower pieces and still lifes. He enjoyed the discipline, and it taught him much about colour and its management. It also bolstered his instinctive restraint, which would not admit distracting accessories such as we see in certain Dutch Masters of still life. In *Dream about a Flower* concentration is intensified by two figurines in close support, both dancers.

> Each facing each as in a coat of arms.[5]

The girl reaches out, reaches up towards the summit of the flower; the other raises a hand in attentive regard. Legs wide apart, he appears to have stopped in mid-dance to extol the flower. His partner, the aspiring girl, approaches the towering bloom on tiptoe. Thus the figurines justify the title, *Dream about a Flower*, through their kinship with Blake's Virgin and Youth in the poem *Ah! Sun-flower* who aspire to 'that sweet golden clime' of innocent sexuality, the dreamt-of, desirable state whose emblems are Blake's sunflower and Weight's passionate red bloom.

In *Edna in her Ball-Gown* (c.1938, page 26) the sensual is a pronounced, a gracious informing element. It followed *Dream about a Flower* by some two years.

I was privileged to bring the artist's attention to the work, which he had not seen for many years. As he brought the slide into focus in the viewer, he gasped slightly as if with satisfied recognition of an early achievement, and as if the pressures productive of the work moved him again *'With throbbings of noontide'*.[6]

Speaking to Norman Rosenthal of his visits to the National Gallery, Carel Weight said that he felt closest to the Flemish portraits, and he singled out one portraitist, Rogier van der Weyden. But at this early stage there is little of Rogier's cool austerities in Edna's portrait! The *estilo frio* is not to appear for nearly fifty years – in, for example, the Kitsons' double portrait (1978, page 99) and the *Portrait of an Actor-Poet* (1979, page 97).

But now Edna, having bought a lovely chiffon gown, invites him expressly to paint her in the manner and mood of a Fragonard.[7] You can see what that means, obviously. The dress *décolletée*, the glowing expanse of flesh above the breasts, the sensuously turned shoulders, the legs visible through the chiffon – all these are features comfortably belonging to a Fragonard. She reaches out – as if to point the eroticism of the work – and grasps with her right hand the neck of a Pre-Columbian *zemi*.[8] It is ithyphallic. With the left, she presses to her lap a tail of the silk girdle which draws the bodice in tightly under the breasts.

The figure is firmly outlined, the curves delicately yet boldly traced; the legs impress their fine shapes into the long, diaphanous skirt. The girdle is tied in a bow at the left, and here the curves lose their precision.

Hogarth – too often dismissed as an authority on aesthetics – is worth citing:

> Some parts of dress should be loose and at liberty to play into foulds some of which will
> be alway winding as the body moves. Nay it is some times proper to contrive things to
> rest in winding forms.[9]

In 'looseness' and 'liberty' Hogarth implies that beauty in dress is enhanced by subtle irregularities – features which here so graciously take the eye.

The flesh tones are gently relieved by a curtain of silvery patterned fabric. It matches the slightly darker shade of Edna's dress, the folds of which are echoed in its irregular fluting. Its flower motifs float behind her – greenery breaking into red blooms. The face is flushed with health, the blue eyes pensive, as if visualising the soft fields and skies of her native Ireland. It is as if Weight had sprung into maturity as a portraitist at the very outset. He was twenty-seven at the time, many years before he was to make any revelation to Rosenthal or myself. It is a personal view – but it has distinguished support – that nothing in Weight's portraiture is superior to this work of sixty years ago.

**Balloon Trip to the Moon** (*c*.1933)
*Oil on board 23 × 15in (58.4 × 38cm),*
*private collection (photograph by courtesy*
*of the Fine Art Society, London).*

**Dream about a Flower (1933)**
*Oil on canvas, 32 × 20in (81.2 × 50.8cm),*
*John Brandler collection / Christie's Images.*

**Edna in her Ball-Gown (c.1938)**
*Oil on canvas, 30 × 24in (76.2 × 60.9cm),*
*private collection.*

When I sent him a photograph of it he phoned to thank me, commenting on the eroticism of the work. 'It really is quite something, isn't it?' he said. 'I think I might have been wrong not to have done more in that line.'

I nervously muttered the Hardy quotation 'Throbbings of noontide.' Weight corrected me abruptly: 'Ah, but I'm not half the man Hardy was!'

The power and charm of Edna's portrait might well have persuaded him to do 'more in that line'. But his art moved unpredictably to impulses peremptory and immediate. Such promptings were prelude to revelation and visionary progress.

He had painted Edna[10] three years earlier (*Edna*, opposite). Here no longer the grand lady in daring formal dress, she wears a simple afternoon frock, and listens and smiles on the threshold of a laugh. She edges forward a little in her chair, quickening to a pleasantry, ready with some spontaneous rejoinder. It is such a slight movement, requiring the stress of the slanting chair and the teacup and saucer tilting in her lap.

It is a cluttered corner in which she sits, the façade of a large dolls' house behind her. She sits at the very apex of the corner, with a complex of lines urging her to the forefront of the picture. The many coloured oblongs of the dolls' house and the flowered cushion at her back introduce, in diminished tones, the vividly coloured figure of Edna in the foreground. In this way these lines and angularities are functional, but they are so numerous that we can only suspect symbolism. They could just be taken to refer to straightforward

**Edna (1935)**
*Oil on canvas, 36 × 28in (91.4 × 71.1cm),*
*private collection.*

**The Thames, Chiswick 1938 (1938)**
*Oil on canvas, 28 × 36in (71.1 × 91.4cm),*
*Walker Art Gallery, Liverpool.*

character, girlish still and of clear intelligence: herself, a little crowded, as it might be, by many engagements and social obligations. But now – she must mind the teacup, or 'it's destroyed she is, surely!'

The few months preceding the outbreak of World War II left little time for more than one major landscape. There were also small-scale portraits and domestic scenes.

One of these was a picture of his mother at her sewing machine, the very symbol of stability as she sits at her unfailing chore. The large round table, the room at evening under the electric light, proclaim an order that 'will go onward the same'.[11]

The major landscape – actually a riverscape – is *The Thames, Chiswick* 1938 (above). We discussed this at the beginning of the chapter, but it warrants a second and closer look.

A few figures, scattered in a rough triangle, assist the scene crucially. There is a languor about them which is in keeping with the waning afternoon and the river arrested by the inflooding waters of the distant estuary. The surface is mirror-smooth where the wide-sweeping arc turns its course out of the picture. Movement is sensed via the lines that point the withdrawal of the man on the left. He, too, is moving slowly away, round the corner where the park railings twist in a counter-curve to that of the river. The birches cast moving shadows on the road, and at the same time hold down the eye upon the static, mirror-like arc of water.

At the apex of the triangle, a small figure in silhouette against the bright mirror marks the point where the river changes direction. Not only that – he is the gnomon indicating the low sun, giving the scene its brief, autumnal life.

What appears at first a straightforward river scene does, in fact, reflect the essential suspense of the season in the mass of water held in momentary stasis. The characters, in their several dispositions, are as dynamic markings in the grander scale of the composition.

For the past seven years (1932–39) Carel Weight had taught at the Beckenham School of Art. But now war intervened with other claims on his sensibility.

# 3

# EXPERIENCE OF WORLD WAR II

———————————— • ————————————

### 1939–43: AS TROOPER AND SAPPER

Carel speaks with satisfaction of only few pictures painted through the troubled shifts of these years. 'What a waste of time!' – thus his summary dismissal. He gratefully acknowledges Sir Kenneth (later Lord) Clark as a powerful friend at court. Clark thought him miscast in his military career and, as Chairman of the War Artists' Advisory Committee, got him the occasional job for the War Office.

Early in May 1941 he had written to Professor Gleadow, founder of the Advisory Committee, to apply for work with the East Coast convoys. How the venture would have affected his art is matter for speculation. Turner in the tempest, lashed to the mast, comes to mind, but Sir Kenneth was able to interest him in something more immediate and arranged that he should paint a picture of the bombing in a suburban district 'with people going about their daily affairs despite the Blitz'.

Meanwhile, Weight carried on teaching at Beckenham – a very happy School where the dominant figure was Henry Carr, a product of the RCA.

> He'd fought all through World War I, and we were very, very friendly. He was a sort of father figure to all the students. I had a say in recommending him to Sir Kenneth Clark, whose idea was to commission someone to paint the portraits of the allied generals. Carr set to on Eisenhower and so on. . . In a way it spoilt Carr, who afterwards became obsessed with grand people. Anyway, he was a lovely man.

For the next two years – before his 'papers' arrived – Weight travelled daily between Beckenham and his home in Shepherd's Bush, in the course of which he saw much that was worthy of his compassion and art.

It was a long, risky train journey – some twenty miles and, at the height of the Blitz, often interrupted by enemy action. Once, as he returned from a visit to someone in Tooting his trolleybus was singled out for attack by a fighter-bomber. The plane swooped at full throttle, but then, 'The pilot decided we weren't worth powder and shot, and made off.' Panic ensued. He was in a front seat, and in the *sauve-qui-peut* the bus was choked with escaping passengers. For a while Weight was sole occupant of the bus. A picture resulted, and was submitted to a Mr E.M. Dickey of the Ministry of Information and Secretary to the War Artists' Advisory Committee. Unfortunately, the painting was rejected: it did not conform closely enough to the subject originally proposed. 'And besides,' Weight added, 'it wouldn't do for British people to be seen in a state of panic.' To the notice of rejection, Dickey kindly added some encouraging advice: 'I hope this will not be a disappointment to you and that you will be ready to have another go.'

It was not like Carel Weight, the compulsive practitioner, to be put off from 'having another go'. Almost immediately he was at work on *Summer Night by the Shelter, Lewisham*. It was at the end of August 1941 and, thanks to Dickey's representation to the appropriate Ministry, Carel Weight's call-up was deferred to allow him to finish his *Lewisham Shelter*. Meanwhile, his trolleybus painting, entitled *It Happened to Us*, was exhibited in a makeshift gallery in the tube station at Charing Cross and met with much popular approval.[1] Dickey wrote on 2 October to say how delighted he was 'to see the good notices of the Show at Charing Cross', referring to the trolleybus subject as having been 'much appreciated'. By 6 November the *Lewisham Shelter* had been accepted by the Advisory Committee.

Weight wrote to Dickey the following explanation:

> The subject of my picture is a shelter in the Lewisham district. I came upon it one warm moonlight late summer evening. The women were sitting outside on chairs peacefully knitting and gossiping with the men. Here were people who had suffered much finding relaxation under war conditions. In contrast were the strident cries of the children not yet put to bed and the ever-restless searchlights swinging in the sky.

**The Battle of Suburbia (1940)**
*Oil on board, 25 × 30in (63.5 × 76.2cm),*
*Leeds City Art Gallery.*

Sadly, the painting did not survive the war. Weight, recently discussing the loss, revealed his sharp and enduring regret. 'I was sad about that. All the other pictures about the war were blown up when the bomb hit my studio.'

One he particularly liked was 'rather satirical' – a crowd of frightened-looking people gawping up at a poster which was telling them how wonderful they were to be carrying on under the conditions of the Blitz. The destruction of that he also regretted. 'It was a pity, because that was a good one.' Then, after a slight pause, as if recovering: 'But, anyway, we've lost a hell of a lot of things better than that.'

His *Battle of Suburbia* seems to have been painted earlier, some time late in 1940, but was not accepted by the Advisory Committee until 5 March, 1942. He may have delayed submitting the work for some reason, or perhaps the Committee was dilatory. He was paid twenty guineas. He wrote to Dickey on 10 March expressing his pleasure with the Committee's purchase of the work, adding this explanation:

> The picture was inspired by my daily journeys down to Beckenham during the Blitz. I
> had in mind the district around Lewisham which suffered terribly. The scene is not an
> actual place.

A three-storey block confronts us end-on. Ripped open by high explosive, its central party-wall and upper floors display a huge double cross. The motif, on a lesser scale, is taken up by the lamppost, whose ladder-rest is the transom which it extends over the long, squat line of terrace roofs in the background. Here and there a face looks through a splintered window upon a familiar world transformed, gutted and exposed. A mantle of cloud – it could be of smoke, for it is tinged red – lowers as if to overwhelm the redemptive image of the streetlamp. A boy stands sentinel with his make-believe rifle at the 'easy'. On the right by the shelter a little girl is protesting vigorously as a boy pulls her hair. In these preoccupations the children sustain the title *The Battle of Suburbia*. The painting hangs in the City Art Gallery, Leeds.

Two officials of the Civil Defence confer on the left. Another man, perhaps sorrowfully, prepares to leave the scene by the pathway which the lamp clearly defines. Dead centre of the picture a girl in dark brown – her approximation to mourning – carries a wreath. Bricks, half-bricks, litter and debris lie around her – the shattered foliage of war. Hers is a tender, human touch in, literally, the heart of this stark, male-dominated scene.

'On the whole,' says Carel Weight, 'I resented the war years. I was fed up with what had happened from my point of view, artistically. So I don't care much for the pictures in the Imperial War Museum.'

Here I intervened to mention *The Recruit's Progress* as something he surely approved. 'I liked that, yes – and I liked another of the escaped zebra.'

*(Panel 1)*

*(Panel 2)*

*(Panel 3)*

*(Panel 4)*

His attitude was not unlike Stanley Spencer's on the outbreak of World War I. Both artists viewed the event as hostile to their calling, Weight with more justification than Spencer, for his studio was bombed and much important material was lost. Spencer's spiritual gain was incalculable, Burghclere deriving from the war as the culmination of his whole artistic life.

'Still,' said Weight, 'one or two things weren't too bad, I suppose.'

*The Escape of the Zebra from the Zoo during an Air Raid* (1941, above) was his favourite, in Mervyn Levy's view 'his best war painting'. Four episodes, in separate panels, show various stages of the event. But after their purchase the panels were rearranged incorrectly, so that Panel 1 was set above Panel 2 at the left, with Panel 3 above Panel 4 on the right. I am taking them here in the sequence originally intended by the artist.

Throughout the panels, a red or blackened sky denotes the weight of the bombardment during which a bomb demolished the Zebra House

> killing a number of the poor beasts. Some of the survivors, in a state of frenzied panic, raced wildly about the Zoo, and one – and this is the central theme of my series of pictures – got out on to the main road and galloped down to Camden Town pursued by the keepers. . . I was asked [by Sir Kenneth Clark] to document this dramatic event, which I did by talking to a number of eyewitnesses for reconstructing the scenes from their accounts of what had happened.

The animal shies at the collapsing buildings and three points of soaring flame which threaten to enclose him. Overhead, and lowering upon the fringe of trees, against which the zebra stands out vivid and beautiful in his

**The Escape of the Zebra from the Zoo during an Air Raid (1941)**
*Four panels, 8 × 13in (20.3 × 33cm), Manchester City Art Galleries.*

terror, the sky rages with the ferocity of the night. A splendid, solitary creature is overwhelmed by alien forces of destruction (Panel 1).

The foreground enclosure is a compound of fire. Between this and the long glazed aviary at the back, the distracted animal races about seeking escape. In the façade of the aviary his image is enlarged and distorted – a dramatic shadow-play of the true dimensions of the animal's terror (Panel 2).

He finds the streets. The shops and pub seem on the point of catching fire. Across crimson streets, his pursuers send their shadows after him. Sharply defined against the ugly blocks, he dashes off at full stretch. In contrast, the officials are blurred, clumsy, hurrying figures, and the superintendent's Austin 7 that staggers to the scene completes a picture of ludicrous incapacity (Panel 3).

**Helen (1938)**
*Oil on board, 33½ × 22½in (85.5 × 57.5cm),*
*Jeffrey and Catherine Horwood collection.*

The last scene is designed to balance the pattern of the panel above (Panel 2). In the built-up space between terraces the zebra, hemmed about by keepers and still dangerously distrusting, is soon to be taken and brought back to Regent's Park. His energies are exhausted and freedom is virtually over (Panel 4).

It is a bravura passage, in which the zebra and its elemental colours are in strident counterpoint to the fire and the darkness of night. A rhetoric, in the appropriate high pitch, is controlled by the refinements of composition, which are of balanced action and nicely complemented patterns. Static and explosively active ingredients provide delicately adjusted nuances, which heighten the emotional shock of the four panels when looked at as a single unit. Sir Kenneth Clark judged it ideal for Weight's sense of the dramatic, and clearly he was right.

Not so military bureaucracy, whose wayward logic drafted Carel Weight into the Royal Armoured Corps. As 7946320 Trooper Weight, CVM, he was put through his basic training at Warminster. His letter to Dickey (already quoted), expressing his delight at the Advisory Committee's purchase of *The Battle of Suburbia*, ended dolefully: 'I am not enjoying myself here. I am not mechanically minded and find everything very difficult.' Then – with the quick sympathy of the artist – he adds: 'On the other hand I get on very well with my companions.'

Some three weeks later Helen Roeder took up arms on his behalf. She wrote to Dickey on 4 April 1942:

> The other day Carel, who is at present engaged in washing greasy mess-tins for 12 hours a day, wrote to me suggesting that he was longing to paint a series of pictures called *The Recruit's Progress*. He says there is a lot to paint in the army if only one were allowed the time. . . and he thinks that now that he has no real work to do but 'fatigues' while he is awaiting his transfer, they might allow him time off if the War Artists' Committee were to ask his CO to do so. I think and expect you will agree with me that he could probably produce some very exciting work for such conditions, as painting the rather Hogarthian scenes in the Army is particularly suited to his talent.[2]

Dickey lost no time in bringing Miss Roeder's representation to Sir Kenneth Clark's notice. But whatever manoeuvres Sir Kenneth adopted passed through the 'normal' channels; nothing materialised, and in late August Weight was moved, and bleak militarised Salisbury Plain was exchanged for the grander bleakness of the North Yorkshire moors and the concentrated militarism of Catterick Camp.

Life was terrible. For Carel Weight, as a relatively older man, PT was a great trial, and the mature artistic spirit was alien to the ultimate perfection of army life – the disciplined conformity to King's Regulations. It was in the very air he breathed. It emanated from the endless lines of huts, eloquent of the military habit of perfection which every soul was constrained to wear. As for art – this enormous imposition upon Nature killed any imaginative stirrings at birth. But Nature had her own poetry.

Whenever Weight could stretch and relax and look beyond his immediate surroundings, then he was uplifted – momentarily. He wrote to Helen Roeder on 12 September 1942:

> The whole countryside has a beauty which is really astonishing. It is hardly England as we know it. Everything is on the grand scale, fine hills, huge trees. I believe Turner painted here and it is he that one is constantly reminded of. O for my oils and some time to work! As it is I am now digging the officers' mess garden, which is quite pleasant after a horrid bout in the kitchen.[3]

Besides bouts of 'spud-bashing', blanco-ing for inspections and guard duties, painting signs and boards ('they love charts and indicators in the Army'), Weight was camouflaging tanks and lorries, then digging them out of ditches and snowdrifts.

But Catterick had its oases. He reports

> a dazzling change of fortune. I was sent for by the CO at the Officers' Mess, and greeted with: 'Mr Speight, I hear you are an RA.' I modestly replied that although I had occasionally shown in that institution I had not that honour.
>
> 'Anyway, I'm told you are an artist . . . Can you work realistically as well?'

# The Recruit's Progress (1942)

**The Medical Inspection**
*Oil on canvas, 20 × 32in (50.8 × 81.2cm),*
*Imperial War Museum.*

**Preparations for an Evening Out**
*Oil on canvas, 20 × 27in (50.8 × 68.5cm),*
*Imperial War Museum.*

**Arms' Drill**
*Oil on canvas, 20 × 27in (50.8 × 68.5cm),*
*Imperial War Museum.*

**An Evening Out – Pub Scene**
*Oil on canvas, 20 × 27in (50.8 × 68.5cm),*
*Imperial War Museum.*

'Yes,' I said meekly.

'Can you do anything like these?' he said, producing a mass of cuttings of rude girlies from *La Vie Parisienne*, *The Bystander*, etc. 'My idea is a lovely scene in Honolulu – dusky girls, sunny umbrellas. . . surf-bathing, so that my officers, after being out in the freezing Yorkshire wind will be able to relax and bathe in the sunshine of Honolulu.'

A month or so later he lands the 'nice job of decorating the Church Room with Saints. . . From Honolulu to Heaven!'

Three days later 'came a sudden reversal of fortune'. The Colonel had been transferred and Weight was told that

> whereas Colonel Broome was all for dancing girls, Colonel Blaine, the new CO, intimated that he wanted a landscape, so he directs the painter to remove the figures. Well, as the whole scheme was designed for figures which were life-size a slight problem presented itself to the artist.
>
> I wonder what Dickens would have said about his publisher if the latter had directed him to remove all the characters from *Pickwick* and enlarge on the descriptions of the English countryside, or Michelangelo, directed by the Pope to remove all the figures from *The Last Judgement*. I have just given up trying to produce anything good and trying to get the bloody thing done.

However, some oases were of pure, unadulterated refreshment. There was a Garrison Symphony Orchestra 'made up entirely of soldiers'. Their concert of Weber, Mozart, Lalo and Brahms he thought 'very well chosen'. Then, too, there were concerts of gramophone records, at one of which 'the most interesting and exciting [items] were of some early works by Shostakovich'. Less stimulating was a gramophone recital conducted by 'the new educational sergeant – a humourless, dried-up creature with glasses (rather like me when I come to think of it)'. It was most likely a frosty occasion, and the pleasantry in parenthesis is a poignant inclusion for Helen's entertainment.

Carel Weight paid regular visits to Mr and Mrs Lionel Brett, to whom he'd been introduced by an old friend. Brett[4] was a prominent architect whose lovely home in Richmond – three miles from camp – became a sanctuary for Weight and a few others of similar gifts and interests. But realities deadened and endured. He wrote:

> I don't want to settle down to this colourless, unproductive life. And I find myself intensely lonely with thousands of faces round, thousands of voices yelling obscenities. . . I cannot find any point of contact with about ninety per cent of them. I am really rather limited, I suppose, my only topics of conversation are Art, people perhaps, and a little politics, nature.

Then he changes key:

> There are a few nice people. . . I was lucky with the Instructor at the Mechanical School who was most intelligent and had a great sense of humour.

With fellow spirits like his Instructor and his special army friends – George Pennell and Ted – Weight would make the most of his free time. A Sunday visit to Darlington with George ended with a visit to

> two pubs, the second of which was most amazingly Hogarthian. Aged harlots, ladies in curious neo-Victorian garments, masses of Yorkshire factory men in caps, rather short and bull-froggish, and the whole company singing improper songs, with rollicking choruses which we yelled out with more gusto than musical perfection.

Again at Darlington towards the end of the year, he has 'an amusing time'.

> Visited the local Art Gallery which had a show of Lowry's pictures of life in the Indus-
> trial North. . . Later (with Ted) to a pub. The singing. . . had become a great chorus
> with all the women (Rowlandson at his best) singing bawdy songs in unison.

He entered with abandon into these full-blooded relaxations, whose spirit he captures in the Pub Scene in his *Recruit's Progress* (pages 34–5).

Through all these alarums and excursions Helen Roeder kept him in touch with more civilised London ways. Life there was dangerous enough, and she faced the frustrations of finding accommodation and the irritation of family crises. Her health – never robust – was causing concern, and Weight would counsel her anxiously.

She would help with his mending which he occasionally packed off to her by post, and if the opportunity for painting seemed likely, she would send him the material he requested. He would respond with the monetary help he could manage. In fact, both helped each other through this trying year, in a relationship of mutual support, tender and lifelong.

Nor did his old foster mother ever lose touch, and at Christmas

> Rose, the sweet, sent me a box containing three pieces of mincemeat, a hunk of
> Christmas pud and some toffees, so I got some Christmas fare, after all.

She had enclosed a letter, telling him that she had 'cut the cards' for him. 'She tells me the war is going to last another year. . . I am going to have quick unexpected changes, but my position will improve.'

Her clairvoyance was remarkably accurate. Even in the sharpest outcry against his loneliness, he acknowledges the intelligence and sense of humour of his Instructor. And, at last, it dawned on the Controlling Powers of the Driving and Mechanical Wing (RAC) that Trooper Weight was not likely to qualify either as Driver or Mechanic. He wrote on 12 November:

> I nearly killed my Instructor yesterday when we drove into another lorry. [This crime
> was not punished.]

Though, in the same letter, he tells Miss Roeder that he was given three days CB for being without PT kit on parade! Such was the Army's practice of justice that a sense of humour was an indispensable commodity.

It seemed more than likely that Rose's prediction would speedily be realised. On 1 January 1943, only ten days after her 'cutting the cards', Weight received 'a delightful letter from K [Sir Kenneth Clark]'; he is 'trying to get me a bit of leave to complete my *Recruit's Progress*. Unfortunately I feel the theme has died on me. Still, of course, I shall try to work it up again.'

It was almost a year since Helen's representation that Sir Kenneth Clark's power prevailed, the necessary leave was granted and *The Recruit's Progress* (the ideas and sketches for which originated in 1942) was painted.

A first formality on call-up or enlistment is the medical inspection – the opening scene of *The Recruit's Progress*. What precisely we are looking at is, in soldierly terms, a 'short arms' inspection' – ie an inspection of the private parts. This accounts for the coyness of the recruit on the right. An orderly remonstrates with him, but with a shielding hand clapped to his flies, he guards his scruples about displaying his nudity. In contrast, the others, half-naked, queue up behind one of their brother recruits who, with trousers rolled down to his ankles, confronts the MO stark-scrotum-naked – to refine a military vulgarism. At the extreme left another steps out of the frame, drawing on his trousers with a shade of dubiety on his face as he ponders the outcome of the inspection.

The next stage in *The Progress* shows them making ready for an evening out, a first taste of freedom. Weight recollects: 'The first months of my military career were absolutely awful. One was bullied by sergeants and all sorts of people, and I disliked it intensely.' Here, under the exhortation of such a sergeant, they bustle into their clothes, having shaved and washed in cramped and speedy discomfort. A powerfully built man titivates himself in a mirror, held steady by a timid-looking lad – no doubt bullied into the job. Respect for authority has lent wings to the diffident lad's dispatch. He alone is fully dressed and ready. The scene is splendidly animated, action and concern are nicely distinguished; the bold, expressive forms could owe something to the Burghclere *Ablutions*.

**Veronese Night (1945)**
*Oil on canvas, 20 × 24in (50.8 × 60.9cm),*
*Imperial War Museum.*

Parade, the third subject of the sequence, takes the form of arms' drill, and the hero, indistinguishable from his companions in the previous episodes, emerges from anonymity to display an ineptitude which wounds the sergeant's professional susceptibilities. With outraged exasperation and outflung, threatening arm, the sergeant points to the affront – a tardy response to his word of command. Our Recruit's rifle is at some indeterminate point between the 'slope' and the 'order'. The sergeant's instructive arm is marvellously expressive of menace and reproof.

The parade ground is puddled and drenched, a dark-glistening mirror redoubling the recruits' misery in their alien world. Above that rainy belt of Catterick a sky, purple with more rain, swags heavy. Behind the sergeant's raw and awkward squad, and misty in the distance, others are marching or receiving similar basic training.

The fourth and last picture of the series is a rumbustious pub scene, full of colour and noise. Christmas decorations – red, green and blue bunting – stretch from wall to wall. The garish wallpaper of red roses and daubed greenery on a yellowish ground is an uneasy backcloth to the violent scene raging in the lower left-hand corner. It could be that the Recruit is quarrelling with the portly fellow we saw earlier studying himself in the mirror. The corner is loud with challenge, flying tankards and bottles spilling from the table as the hero bids to rescue his girl, protesting and struggling in the enemy's embrace. A friend, moderating, restrains the hero in a well-intentioned but clumsy intervention, the result of which is to up-end the table and throw the second lady in the party from her chair. She casts a shocked expression at us as she passes from view. It is all we glimpse, save her shoulders and upflung legs which, sharply angled to her unseen body, are lines of force, dynamics of her bottoming-out.

In short, a fine old barney, evoking a rich variety of response from pretty well all the other patrons. The theme is Hogarthian, a crowd scene of noisy animation in a robust Bruegelian vein. Although the invitation to laugh is irresistible, we recognise at the same time – as with a Bruegel – the painter's first concern for truth: here, the harsh realities of the recruit's tragi-comical position.

There was nothing else in quite the same class, despite Weight's declaring there was 'a lot to paint in the army'. Conditions were adverse. And, as we have seen, it was a struggle against the odds to paint *The Recruit's Progress*.

'No, on the whole I was rather fed up with what the war had done for my art.' He was thinking particularly of the bombing of his studio, and the loss of so much that was precious to him. So many threads were lost in his development as an artist that, as with Spencer more than thirty years before, he felt thrown out of stride.

But the heavy skies seemed to be lifting. Grim Catterick suggested an amusing finale for his *Recruit's Progress*. A scandal was circulating involving a much-hated sergeant's seduction of an ATS NCO. She, too, was a sergeant, so that there was no case of incompatibility of rank! It prompted a fifth and final panel. The sergeant would be discovered by 'the Idle Recruit who would report him to the CO, who in gratitude, would make him his chief nark and award him a stripe. Thus would redemption and a happy ending conclude the series.'

Again, Rose's predictions were fulfilled when Weight was transferred to the RE's at Ruabon, a border village on the edge of the Vale of Llangollen. To Sapper Weight, the change came as a wonderful relief, not only because of the more congenial surroundings, but in the good fortune of being commanded by an enlightened, cultivated man. Weight was at home immediately in a unit mostly of draughtsmen employed in map-making.[5] He confesses that he was no great success in this, but much was propitious and the colonel 'leant over backwards to give us time off for drawing. Every Sunday he arranged for us to attend an early Church Parade, and then released us for the rest of the day. We all had to go out very early in the morning, but it was wonderful to get in a day's painting.' Of course, his equipment was limited to a small box of watercolours, but by the time he had finished his service with the Unit he had a sufficient portfolio to hold a little exhibition with two or three others in London.

At Ruabon he was able to extend his reading – he picks up a copy of Heine in Wrexham, and enjoys the little essay on Jan Steen which, he thinks, should be a model for the art historian. He forms a lifelong friendship with Pat Gierth, who later succeeds him as a sergeant in the Command College of the Army Education Corps in London. True, the restrictions were still there, and the less sympathetic NCOs with their reverence for footling regulations, but the compensations were adequate. He organised a Unit Art Exhibition at Wrexham, at which Pat Gierth had the distinction of selling the only work. 'There were about two hundred and fifty things exhibited,' wrote Carel Weight, 'not bad for a single Unit.' There were visits to a cosy little pub where the singing was taken seriously, all the patrons listening rapt and discriminating like connoisseurs. And another art show was mounted in Camp, where his *The Red Gloves* '[shone] out and [looked] really lovely'.

It's not surprising that we catch the distinct note of relief. Pat Gierth, who arrived at the place – actually Wynnstay House, Ruabon – some months before Weight, gives this impression: 'There was an amazing avenue of chestnuts going off into infinity with deer all over the place and easels with khaki figures painting away like khaki Van Goghs.'

With understandable optimism, Weight looks forward to a leave and requests Helen to warn her musical friends that he's 'dying to hear them play the Elgar Violin Sonata for my homecoming'.

At last he is able to paint with a freedom undreamt of in Catterick. In one of his Sunday letters he records: 'worked from two o'clock until ten pm, stopping for half-an-hour for tea.' Then – in the same breath – he adds: 'Isn't it grand that Musso has been kicked out?' He can even look forward to his final discharge. 'I wonder how I will feel when I walk out of the Army? What shall I do with myself?' For the moment, life was less burdensome.

He became the subject of a good-natured cartoon in the unit newspaper – in broadsheet format for the noticeboard. He described it for Miss Roeder:

> It shows a company of soldiers who have just turned left, all except one bespectacled creature who has turned right. It has caused an H.M. Bateman situation in which the Commanding Officer is told: 'That's Barel Tate, the famous artist!'

Even military decorum, so sensitive to prejudice, was fraught with farcical potential: 'Nearly a fiasco yesterday when my braces broke on parade. Somehow I was able to pass it off unnoticed.'

But more of those quick, unexpected changes of Rose's prediction were soon to follow, and the year, it seemed, was rounding off nicely. On 30 November 1943 he triumphantly sent Miss Roeder this telegram: 'Chester Interview successful. Accepted AEC. Carel.'

But Christmas failed to put its festive seal on his change of fortune. Instead it was marred by a sorrowful indifference:

> Am annoyed with the family. I haven't received even a Christmas Card from them. It's silly to be annoyed, I know, but when one is living in a hut containing thirty men and only one electric light, one gets a bit touchy at this time of year.

Sad news had also reached him from Henry, Rose's son. Her eye condition, which had long been troublesome, had worsened, and the eye had to be lost to save the sight of the other. Weight's bald statement of the fact in his letter conceals nothing of his reaction to the cruel irony that such a sacrifice was demanded of his sweet, his clear, spiritually sighted Rose.

### 1944–46: AS SERGEANT AND CAPTAIN

Carel Weight was duly transferred to the Army Education Corps with the rank of sergeant, and took over the art department of their Command College in Queen's Gate.

Work was congenial but uphill. Administrative arrangements were often frustrated, and teaching suffered constant disruption from the removal of pupils for military duties and fatigues. Nor was his new colonel the sympathising commander he had left in Wales – but at least he was back in London, where the Advisory Committee might keep him under closer view.

However, it was not until 18 January 1945 that the Committee wrote offering him the important assignment of recording 'some aspects of the big ordnance catastrophe at Hereford'.[6] The proposal was that he 'should be asked to do a reconstruction painting of the tragedy, and also a group of the heroes of the occasion'. The Committee offered 35 guineas for the work; Third Class travel was allowed, together with a personal allowance of £1 and 6s 8d for more than a ten hours' absence from home. In those days it was magnanimity itself. Permission was sought from the CO at the beginning of the following week.

Mr Dickey had been replaced as Secretary to the Committee, but his successor, Mr Colin Coote, continued to be every bit as supportive. He wrote on 23 January 1945:

> We should very much like the benefit of his fine powers of recording. I do not think he would need more than a month to undertake this work. . . I should be very glad to know if we can have your kind co-operation.

Whatever the real reasons, the colonel replied on 3 February 1945:

> It is very much regretted that Sgt Instructor Weight cannot be permitted to undertake the commission you suggest.
>
> He is paid from Army funds to work in a full-time capacity and he is only entitled to four periods of nine days' privilege leave annually and consideration of compassionate leave if domestic circumstances warrant.
>
> Continued absence for one month, therefore, is absolutely inadmissible.

Small wonder that Weight remains to this day resentful of what the war had done for his art. And, despite his promotion from the Education Corps to the appointment of Official War Artist with the rank of captain, and the opening of wider horizons in the larger European theatre, his most telling war paintings were done before his putting on khaki, within the familiar purlieus of London.

As an Official War Artist he produced an immense corpus of work. In a letter to Miss Roeder in November 1945 he tells her that he hopes 'to have completed about sixty pictures' by the end of the year.

He pushed himself hard, but made time to attend the Italian opera, the concert and ballet. In Vienna he took the like advantage of his hours off duty. His sight-seeing was responsible – to sense the atmosphere of a scene, the habits and life of the people. His walk in the Vienna woods in autumn was restorative and, inwardly refreshed, he was better able to fulfil the demands of his commission.

The apparatus of modern war was of less interest to Weight than the way war affected the human being.

His several harbour scenes are adequate as a record, but where humanity is absent the work lacks the vital appeal of art. An expansive landscape, with sketchy human figures swamped by the scale of the subject, amounts only to direct reporting. I have seen such works in reproduction only, so that when they become more accessible than they are at present, these comments will need reappraisal. Many of these pictures are widely dispersed, particularly those in the Government Art Collection, and will be abroad in various Embassies and Consulates. Others are in private hands.

This account is therefore compressed to concentrate on items reasonably accessible and generally accepted as Weight's most characteristic work as Official War Artist.

With bewildering suddenness, life became free and fulfilling – so light were the constraints his commission imposed. He was in Naples by the end of May 1945 – in the land of art, the culmination of the upward trend in his fortunes. He reacted with sustained bouts of creativity and immersed himself in the riches of both the Old and later Masters. He was the right man in the right place, and though transport was a great difficulty, he ranged widely over the peninsula, returning to Rome to replenish his equipment and chivvy the REs responsible for crating his pictures for shipment to England. Once refuelled, he was away covering much ground and many subjects.

In Florence, he climbed the scaffolding in Santa Croce as the workmen removed the protecting walls from the Giottos; in a gloomy room – lit only by handlamps – he saw Botticelli's *Primavera*. Perugia offered him Perugino and the Umbrian painters, and from there he travelled to the Giottos and Cimabues in Assisi. The riches of Rome, Milan and Pisa swell the record of his itinerary; the whole inventory is too extensive to itemise.

Unfortunately, the realities of war had first claim on his attention.

In Weight's picture of the *Palazzo Vecchio* (1945, Imperial War Museum, London), concerned and war-weary Florentines stand about or approach the ruins in the Vacchereccia, overlooked by the *palazzo* itself. The venerable building, with the replica of Michelangelo's *David* at its entrance, contrasts ironically with the ruins in the foreground.

The few sightseers register in their several attitudes a shocked, distressed curiosity as they wander along and look at the rubble, once the glorious buildings of the Vacchereccia. And yet there is an impression of resilience in the young mother and her child and the elegantly dressed girl standing in the patch of sunlight, with the tragic rubble at either side.

Frail humanity is of greater symbolic significance than the palace, whose 'defiant fortress-like structure. . . serves to express the power exercised by the Florentine community' (Baedeker, *Florence*, 1990). The tower dominates, its clock counting the steps of the city's history distinguished by moments more worthy of humanity than the passage of modern armies with their legacy of ruin – a legacy which made hazardous the painting of the *Palazzo Vecchio*.

Weight's intention was to show how close the bombing had come to the Palazzo, and he took up a vantage point in a wrecked house in the Vacchereccia. He was working on the second floor when it collapsed beneath him and he fell to the rubble underneath. He escaped with a few bruises: his paintbox was almost a total loss.

There were evenings of leisure, for a change.[7] Work itself could be shelved in favour of the concert, the opera and ballet. He heard Gigli in an open-air *Pagliacci*, and as Don José in *Carmen*. In both cases he had reservations. He thought *Pagliacci* 'marvellously spectacular, though not always in the best of taste. The opera isn't one that should be done in the grand manner. . . *Carmen* was sumptuous, but not very good.'

He is silent, however, on the next day's concert, which might have made up for shortcomings. The programme included '*The Eroica*, the *Siegfried Idyll* and the inevitable *Bolero*.' A performance of the Tchaikovski Fifth, which he attended with Eric Newton, the art historian and critic, was interesting.

> Curiously [it] got both of us. Whether the old barnstormer was very beautifully played, or whether we were just in the right mood I don't know. What is the curious magic of the man? The orchestra was very definitely sympathetic and torrents of lyrical sentiment were poured upon us – and how lovely it was.

The open-air performance in Rome would have something to do with the 'curious magic'. The waltz melody came, after all, from Florence, and the Roman evening would be answerable for additional ingredients of magic.

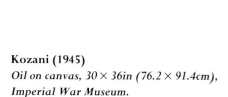

**Kozani (1945)**
*Oil on canvas, 30 × 36in (76.2 × 91.4cm),*
*Imperial War Museum.*

It was a crowded year. *Between Two Fires: A Dream* (1945)[8] belongs to an early spell in Rome and Weight, with justification, dismisses the work as inconsiderable.

He made sad expeditions to Verona and Rimini – both tragically devastated – writing to a Mr Gregory of the Advisory Committee on 21 September 1945 that his ruined street in Florence and a Verona street scene were 'of better quality' than anything he'd sent in his 'first batch'.

In *Veronese Night* (1945, page 38) citizens, seated about an ornamental pond, are determined to throw off gloom and enjoy the first days of their 'new life' as fully as straitened circumstances allow. Their humanity informs the scene. A runnel flows from the pond under a ruined bridge to border a distant piazza, where a crowd gathers to chatter with characteristic excitement. The impedimenta of the classical past, or busts of recent dignitaries, observe the scene from their terms.

In the centre, a ragged child is begging with her hand held out to the Scottish soldier who has just entered from the left. His hand in the pocket of his shorts explores its contents. A young girl draws near with a tiny baby, its face like a pink rose at the neck of her thin frock. Tension is evident in the triangle of interests broadly stated by the begging child and the young woman aware of the soldier sounding the well of his resources.

The sunset flares in distant windows and flushes against the dark clouds as if to arrest the oncoming night, of which the clouds give earnest. After all, it is a magic name, Verona, and perhaps the connotation of a famous passion hovers, paled down, in the heart of the tawdry young woman with the pink 'rose' at her breast.

Weight attached this note to the picture:

> I have attempted to give the essence of a summer evening in the city. It is similar in
> most aspects to any North Italy town which has suffered through the war.[9]

The conformity would account for his dissatisfaction with most of his war pictures. Bombed sites, one after the other, proved so monotonous as to deaden his response, and the burdened atmosphere the war left over the ruins was heavy and dispiriting.

Nor was this the only reason. Too often it was a case of enforced reporting. For example, he felt he should paint the room in Caserta where the German capitulation had taken place – 'they might like that'. As it happened, the room was 'unpictorial', and he jibbed, despite being spurred by a strong sense of duty.

By the middle of October he was in Vienna. 'Poor Vienna, with its derelict stucco palaces, its ruined St Stephen's (the marvellous gothic steeple is intact) and its hungry, poverty-stricken people.'

Besides visiting Schoenbrunn, the Emperor's summer residence, and walking in the Vienna woods ('the autumnal colours and the soft air made one feel horribly sentimental'), he went other, more hazardous rounds.

> The set-up was exactly like the film *The Third Man*. . . I used to wander about at night and go straight through the Russian lines. I would wave at the sentries and they always used to wave back; and when the CO said 'Where have you been?' I described it and he said, 'It's a wonder you weren't killed.'[10]

Listening to such an account, we hear the measured voice of the calm man on the threatened trolleybus, and recognise the quality that urged him to volunteer for work on the East Coast convoys. And, characteristically, he is absolute in disclaiming any vestige of heroism.

It had become wintry, almost too wintry to paint the *Razumovski Palace* (1945), despite its association with Beethoven and its power to conjure up the glittering patronage of those eponymous string quartets. Now, on a bleak afternoon, it intensified in poignant irony the sorry scene in the foreground. A few folk, bewildered by the occupation of the Allied armies, stand about in idle, spiritless chatter. Others are moving with an appearance of determination. A group, dwarfed by the pillars of the massive portico, observes two women laying claim to a scrap of firewood. Their dog prances around, excited by the prospect of a little comfort.

Carel Weight found Vienna 'stimulating, more so than Rome – in spite of the wretched, run-down state of the city'. Musical events were numerous, almost wholly excellent. There was, for instance, 'a marvellous performance of *Fidelio*, and it was a tremendous thrill. The audience was the most cosmopolitan I have ever seen. Most of all were Russians in their magnificent medals and braid.' He attended the opera twice in the same week in November when 'the great thrill was *Tosca*. What a lovely work it is. Had no idea!'

Weight wrote to Gregory on 2 January 1946 that, having sent him two crates of pictures, he was 'off to Athens for a short time next week'. It was an exciting prospect, and he wrote to Miss Roeder like a man inspired: The mountains look on Marathon and Marathon looks on the sea. Whoopee![11]

The reality was a disappointment. He reached Athens on a bleak afternoon to find the city in darkness, paralysed by a strike which had closed the power station. Somehow he settled in quite quickly, minus the usual creature comforts. 'To ask for warm shaving water in the morning is simply not done [he was in the Cosmopolitan Hotel]. I am, however, sometimes brought a cup of tea and I often shave in that.'

The weather was alternately severe and benign. On 2 February 1946 he wrote to Miss Roeder: 'I have been working hard for the past week, sometimes freezing, sometimes becoming quite lethargic in the warmth.'

This was the last stage in his Odyssey, and it resulted in two very considerable works – the second of these, *Kozani*, is in my view the most distinguished painting of his entire career as Official War Artist. The first was *Athens: A Typical Street*, a sombre scene overall, but one of varied movement and interest. A small child in red dashes to embrace her mother. With arms outspread, she offers a colourful, spirited touch as foil to the drab knots of people – idle or gossiping in the ruined street. It is a telling evocation of a people dispirited after four years of war, enemy occupation and fighting between rival partisan groups.

Two years before Weight's visit, ELAS (the People's Liberation Army) had attempted to take Athens in a bid to seize political power. Order was restored by the British Forces, but tragically after heavy fighting with ELAS. Weight's description:

> A typical street in Athens which suffered considerably in the ELAS fighting. The damaged building at the end of the street was the last ELAS stronghold. The streets are always thronged with people – men standing at street corners – black marketeers doing their business without restraint. . . I think I have achieved a balance between a good painting and a good historical record.

A couple are coming away from the scene towards us, the man listening perfunctorily to his wife's chatter. Two Orthodox priests are also leaving. In close conversation, and steeped in their own affairs, they are totally

**The Tired Soldier (1943)**
*Drawing.*

isolated from everyone else. Two partisans – one in British uniform – meet for an exchange of war experiences. Any old military scrap was service dress for the partisan forces of those days.

Before the end of the week Weight was busy with a similar subject – a drab, ravaged street with pedestrians as anxious hurrying pairs or as scattered individuals, bewildered and tense. Some are gathering near the corner entrance to a large building in the distance which could be a bank. At the near corner on the left, where an arrest is apparently being made, a few pause to observe from a safe distance. Their interest is cursory and distracted, as if the event were too commonplace to command attention.

During his first morning in Athens, Weight had sought advice of the Press Attaché at the Embassy. This turned out to be Osbert Lancaster, who now arranged for him to visit the 'wilds of Northern Macedonia . . . with an officer who had to visit the region'.

Two days of bumping about in a fifteen hundredweight truck, passing Thebes, Thermopylae and Mount Olympus itself, brought them to their destination, Kozani. He was told later that 'wolves and even bears' might have been encountered on the road, but he 'thought this doubtful, didn't see any, anyway'.

It was some two hundred miles to the north of Athens.

> My companions had come to these remote places to help the Greeks to train their army
> – there is a Greek brigade stationed here. Kozani is an important town – capital of
> Western Macedonia, but to English eyes it would appear very small and poor. The
> houses, however, are most remarkable, they are very like our overhanging Elizabethan
> houses. It was a Turkish town and evidently they contributed this style to architecture.

Here, in Kozani, Carel Weight found a perfect subject in which the human situation was paramount. He viewed it with a compassion which he stated in a powerful, beautiful composition. It is interesting to compare the finished picture with a preliminary sketch in which the women are absent from the balcony in the foreground. They are later, vital inclusions to interpret the painter's attitude.

In presenting the work to the Imperial War Museum, he wrote briefly in explanation:

> British Officers are helping to train the new Greek Army. This is *Kozani* [1945, page 42],
> painted from the top of the British Officers' Mess. In the street [is] a batch of conscripts
> for the Greek Army marching through the town to the barracks. The picture is quite
> colourful – helped by the gaily painted houses.[12]

The perspective is from an elevated point – the top balcony of the Officers' Mess. Its inverted triangular shape determines the arrangement basic to the composition as a whole. The two balcony groups – the three officers and the three women – conform to the same triangular arrangement.

The women, possibly employed as mess servants, are brought as close to the edge of the lower frame as the canvas permits. We read their expressions, anxious or resigned, and allow these to direct our reactions to the men marching below them in the narrow street. In the jutting apex of the balcony, the officers are absorbed with details of administration and, attentive to immediate matters, are little concerned with the women or ourselves.

Enduring Nature provides a lovely theatre for 'this post-haste and romage in the land' – a sky promises soft rain and a mountain range is topped, here and there, with bright powderings of snow.

What, I wonder, was left when all was over, and Carel Weight could at last take stock? Who knows?

> *Infinite passion and the pain*
> *Of finite hearts that yearn—*[13]

These more than ever had become living realities, and more deeply he'd have recognised man's essential loneliness and isolation, even when thronged about like his poor Recruit and Zebra.

# 4

## THE POST-WAR PERIOD
### The Royal College of Art – London Scenes, a Fantasy and Religious Subjects

Carel Weight's life was soon to become doubly energetic – as a practising artist and full-time art tutor. In 1946 he joined the staff of the Royal College of Art. Years earlier, at eighteen, he had won a scholarship to the College which circumstances prevented his taking up – his father was too well off for his son to qualify for the grant. But now the years of distinguished endeavour had brought their reward. He was appointed to the Painting School to teach still life, and it would be wrong to assume that Carel Weight – concerned as he was with depicting movement – would find the concentration on still life anything like a chore. We have to realise that when he first exhibited in the Cooling Gallery in 1933, two-thirds of the paintings were still lifes. He was interested in the challenge, which provided useful exercises in the discipline of close observation.

Weight proved to be a kind, firm and dedicated tutor. In 1949 he initiated the Young Contemporaries show, an exhibition of students' work for the 'exhibition-going public'. It caught on at once, and soon became reputed and influential. And life went on as smoothly as the teaching of art permits, Weight having no difficulty in combining the two strands of his 'doubly energetic life'.

It was an extraordinary period for any Art School. Students formed groups and became the centre of two art movements in this country. They were actually responsible for the second, less successful of these – the so-called Kitchen Sink School, or School of Social Realism, as officially designated. It failed, but in my view, only in the commercial sense. I thought the pictures were remarkable. An exhibition was held in Helen Lessore's gallery. The subjects were depressing, and very little sold. A pity. Some very good work came from people like Bratby, Jack Smith, Peter Coker and a whole lot of others. I thought it far more interesting than the 'Pop' Art which followed, although that was much more marketable. . .

As soon as Robin Darwin took over in 1948 he dressed us down thoroughly. It was a rotten School – he was going to fire the lot of us. We could reapply for reappointment, if that's what we wanted. It was up to us. He and the governors would reconsider our positions. He closed the meeting abruptly. Then he detained me. 'As far as you're concerned,' he said, 'your position's safe. I shall reinstate you.'

Darwin's declared intention was to appoint the strongest possible staff to the Painting School. He wanted it to be the foremost department in the College. I think he succeeded in this. He had John Minton, Ruskin Spear and Rodrigo Moynihan. [Weight omitted himself.] Moynihan was the first Professor, following Darwin's somewhat summary dismissal of Gilbert Spencer. Moynihan was an excellent brain, but he'd so quickly cool off, lose interest and stay away for long periods. So Darwin sacked him and appointed me in his place. It was much against my wishes, and I said so. I was a painter. Administration wasn't my line. But no – it wouldn't do. 'Run the School in the morning,' said Darwin, 'and paint the rest of the day!'

On that basis things went along quite well. It was a huge School of over a hundred students – all excellent and hardworking. Most had experienced military service and were only too delighted to be working at what they most enjoyed. But in four years [1953] things were beginning to change with the arrival of the 'Pop' generation, and in an incredibly short time the entire structure of things changed. Rights became the rage, dissent was rife, mostly irrelevant and ludicrous. I could no longer make decisions without first consulting this or that Union. It had a terrible effect on the less able,

**Holland Walk (c.1946)**
*Oil on canvas, 25½ × 21½in (64.7 × 54.6cm), Hastings Museum and Art Gallery.*

**Holborn Circus (1947)**
*Oil on canvas, 24 × 42in (60.9 × 106.6cm),*
*John Brandler collection/Sotheby's, London.*

middle-of-the-road student. The good ones just got on with the job. Luckily, they were in the majority, and – as far as I was concerned – they saved the day.

He was, even so, quite in sympathy with Pop Art, as its chief concern was with people.

What had gone before was Abstract-Expressionism, and all that seemed a bit inhuman, so I was glad to see anything that had to do with people. Students like David Hockney came along and, whatever you say about him, he did show a very original outlook. I also liked Kitaj,[1] Boshier[2] and all those people.[3]

Later, around 1957, John Bratby was to exhibit with the Young Contemporaries.

He proceeded to turn the place upside-down. He used the life-room for himself and filled it with dustbins from around the back of the V & A, and proceeded to paint himself naked in front of a mirror. Girls would go in and come out screaming.[4]

Darwin wrote of this generation:

The student of 1959 is less easy to teach because the chips on his shoulder, which in some cases are virtually professional epaulettes, make him less ready to learn; yet this refusal to take ideas on trust, though it may not be congenial to the tutor, may in the long run prove to be a valuable characteristic. The students of today are on the whole much more extraordinarily dressed and a lot dirtier and this no doubt reflects the catching philosophy of the 'beat' generation.[5]

Let us take up the other strand in Weight's life – that of the practising artist.

Demobilisation was orderly and slow, and the service uniform was no longer the ubiquitous feature of daily life. Servicemen anticipated their freedom and, like the young man in *Holland Walk* (c.1946, page 45), relaxed in 'civvies' and savoured their 'unhoped-for emancipation'[6].

In the picture, springtime goes forward tardily as if to reflect the quieter, less urgent ordering of life. The copse is still a faint brown, and the greening process is leisurely, even sluggish. A new spaciousness moves the quiet English people to take more than a cursory interest in each other. And a black-and-white terrier, observing us, invites us to take the air of this unaccustomed, peaceful spring.

From a window somewhere in Holborn Carel Weight records the city's stricken face. He looks down on the premises of the *Daily Mirror*, now reduced to the footings of its immense basement. Great creating Nature softens this unsightliness with scattered outbursts of greenery. Two large hoardings, stilted on scaffolding, announce the *Mirror's* claim to the ruined site. They are pinned together like a huge omission-mark, angled to survey the destruction and point directly to the equestrian statue of Prince Albert in the middle of the Circus. Aloft on its plinth, serenely undamaged amid the general wreckage, it testifies, with Dickensian irony, to the significance of grandeur. Did Carel Weight intend any such stricture? Very likely. It was there, ready-made, for the asking.

An imaginative viewer might suppose that *Holborn Circus* (1947, opposite) gaped as if yawning, and flexed itself under the clear sky, whose thin overspread of cloud could disperse at any moment. Citizens chat, window shop, wait at bus stops, line the pavements in patterns which accident determines. Elders are cautiously dressed, young women as colourfully and stylishly as austerity allows. Towering blocks hide St Andrew's gutted church and speak exclusively of commerce. The poignancy which marked the *Palazzo Vecchio* is absent. People drift along or stride purposefully past with scarcely a glance at the devastation. Londoners, inured to the horrors of the Blitz, are resigned to the ugliness of its aftermath.

Weight's 'fine powers of recording' are here exercised in direct and objective reporting. Like the typical *Street in Athens*, it is a balance between historical record and a satisfying picture. It is a powerful exposition of disaster, expansive yet tensioned via the broad, vigorous run of streets and the sharper, arresting uprights. Above all – though we have to look closely to appreciate this – it is a human show of tiny figures who represent the soul of the city recovering breath after the exhaustion of war.

Having so closely recorded the minutiae of destruction, Weight turned westward with relief – to Kensington, which had escaped the worst of the Blitz, and to the *Albert Bridge* (1948). 'I think it one of the loveliest bridges over the Thames,' he said. And indeed it is a uniquely interesting structure, only one other of the type existing in Europe.[7]

No doubt the poet's eye would see all bridges as having commerce with water, earth and air; in the suspension bridge, it should perceive the polarity of massive pressures sustained by the opposing, superior strength of the beautiful and ornate.

A human scene is in progress in the foreground, with tiny figures as living entities animated by their own concerns. They are in telling juxtaposition to the bridge – enhancing its dominance and the significance of the freight passing over its deck.

In conversation, I introduced the subject of *The Good and the Bad Conscience* (1955, above). 'A man and a woman are coming towards us,' Weight explained, 'on a suspension bridge. And they're thinking. One of them – the woman – has her hair pulled by a demon. The man is good, so he's walking along quite happily.'

The occasion was our first meeting, and nervously I ventured the child's question: 'It's not his wife necessarily?'

It evoked a chuckling answer. 'No, no, well. It could be. I don't mind. I don't mind what you make of it!'

He had long realised how the structure of the suspension bridge could serve dramatic ends. Only relate its basic mechanics to some human drama and something remarkable could result. The plunging and lifting catenaries that flank the deck, or 'stage', would impel the actors to the 'proscenium' front and seize the attention of the audience.

**The Good and the Bad Conscience (1955)**
*Oil on canvas, 30 × 25in (76.2 × 63.5cm),*
*Somerset County Museum, Taunton.*

47

**The Return of the Prodigal Son (1947)**
*Oil on canvas, 27 × 36in (68.5 × 91.4cm),*
*John Brandler collection / Sotheby's, London.*

The effect was realised in two paintings, *The Good and the Bad Conscience* and *Fright* (1959). They share the same setting: a tiny suspension bridge near Teddington – a footbridge, actually – which extends a little way across the water to an ait where amateur sailors moor their boats. Hardly a spot where you expect 'things to happen'. But a few Weightian ingredients make conditions propitious for a haunting – the sky flares, the water is tinged pink and lamps on the farther bank gleam through shadowed trees like so many watchful eyes.

> On this evening when actual forms become shadowy and mysterious, thought becomes
> more vivid and concrete. The young girl is tortured by her conscience that pulls
> savagely at her hair. Her companion, with years of experience, wears his with ease, if a
> little smugly.[8]

You may see from this the lively virtues of Carel Weight as a dramatic artist. How wisely chosen is the massive, graceful centrepiece of the bridge, how functional it is in his stagecraft, (i) to promote the action and isolate the actors with their Intelligences, and (ii) to arrest the viewer's attention on the sinister, even Satanic features, via the finials against the sky and the towered 'gateway' against the wood.

The incongruous is as much Weight's formula for wonder as it is for his humour. With the directness of a Flemish primitive, Weight rewards virtue and vice their merited guerdon. The Good is laurel-crowned, the Bad dragged by the hair. He uses the traditional apparatus of divine intervention with the attitude of one who can't take it too seriously – not in this work, at any rate.

Such conflict between awesome effects in nature and the comedy of the human situation show Weight's romanticism at full stretch – a quality numerous reviewers have seized on. With what dutiful address the

demon tears at the woman's hair, and the good angel finds leverage for his weightless foot on the brim of the bowler hat, now due to receive the wreath of virtue!

It is a moment of vision, all right, which Blake would designate a moment of *twofold* vision. For there is the impulse under which it is possible to paint the sky, whose striations could transform – do at times transform – into the powers of the air and make of the buttressed pylons of the bridge a portal to The Dark Wood, with the Thames running red like the Phlegethon of the *Inferno*. And there is a pressure – quite as irresistible – asserted by the daemon of mischief, importunate to reduce pomposity to the ridiculous.

As far back as September 1945, writing to Helen Roeder from Rome, Weight mentions a night scene entitled *The Good Samaritan, Verona* (1945).[9] *Veronese Night* – already discussed – could be so construed, with the Scottish soldier as the Samaritan. But that was essentially a war picture – a nocturne with people relaxing at the end of the day. The 'parable', though in the foreground, is too much part-and-parcel of the general interest to stand out as a religious element in its own right.

In turning to Stanley Spencer's great store cupboard, Weight does produce some Spencer-like effects. In *The Return of the Prodigal Son* (1947, opposite), the plaid suiting of the Prodigal's father, the work-a-day dress of his mother could have been taken from Stanley's wardrobe. And, like Spencer, Weight revels in giving precision to the formal hedgerows and metal railings. A finial is as sharply turned, a hedged enclosure, with its upstanding Michaelmas daisies, as meticulously painted as anything in Spencer.

Against the watery sky, suggesting the nearness of the sea, are the sails, funnels and masts which have returned the Prodigal to his family.

**The Betrayal of Christ (1954)**
*Oil on canvas, 48 × 53in (121.9 × 134.6cm),*
*York City Art Gallery / Royal Academy of*
*Arts Library.*

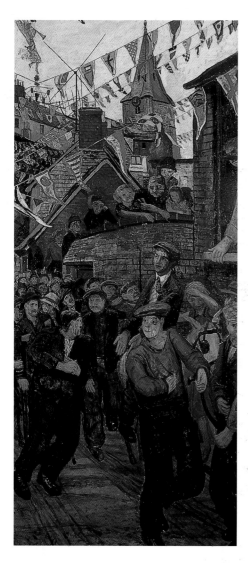

**Entry into Jerusalem (1958)**
*Oil on panel, 86 × 36in (218.4 × 91.4cm),*
*Mr and Mrs Alfred Mignano collection.*

We had spoken briefly of *The Return of the Prodigal Son* when we were discussing *The Thames, Chiswick* 1938. I mentioned the curves and counter-curves in that work, and suggested that similar devices were used in *The Prodigal*.

'I suppose so,' he conceded. However, I felt I was on the wrong tack, and that other, more subtle features had been of greater concern. 'I suppose so – yes,' he repeated, hesitantly. 'But I hadn't thought of it like that. My pictures always have to do with movement. Sometimes to get a feeling of movement, you have to have everything still, and then – just one thing moving – may be a sufficient contrast.'

Above the vigorous curve of the fence and the sheltered, upstanding Michaelmas daisies, the trees take the wind and raise their branches wildly to echo the emotional scene going on underneath. Still more subtle agents are also at work. Father and son embrace under a massive forked tree, symbolic of parting ways; the mother, her plump arms extended towards the embracing men, stands selflessly aloof, to give father and son the full intimacy of their reunion. The elder brother – an obscure face at the window on the left – waits in the wings sourly to play his part.

Weight followed the practice of numerous other Masters, ancient and modern, and gave his religious subjects the cogency of a recognisable contemporary setting. Generally, his inventions preceded his finding their scenes of action. But as a great Londoner, knowing as intimately as Dickens the capital's purlieus – atmospheric, or suggestive of symbolism – Weight found little difficulty in discovering the appropriate setting.

But it was a long, troublesome job finding the place grand enough and cold enough to symbolise the authority directing the arrest and *The Betrayal of Christ* (1954, page 49). The search was rewarded when he found, complete to the toppling urn, the classical terrace in Crystal Palace Park, Sydenham.

We have seen in *The Good and the Bad Conscience* (page 47) how an essentially serious subject tempts Weight to give rein to his sense of humour. The religious subject seldom escapes some lighthearted inclusion, often quietly amusing, even broadly farcical. In this he is not 'playing safe', avoiding the sublime, by deliberately crossing that slim line between high seriousness and its opposite – he is allowing the capricious humour of life to appear perversely where it is inappropriate. Thus, in the action in the foreground of *The Betrayal of Christ*, the kiss, calmly delivered by Judas, coarsened yet poised in his treachery, contrasts with the agitated figures cringing behind the arresting soldiers. The packed group is in a tensed-up state, with the Lance-Corporal not too effectively in control.

A huge marble urn topples on its plinth, an allusion to the destruction of the temple and the imminent collapse of classical values. At the foot of the plinth the servant of the High Priest kneels in the agony of his severed ear. He clasps his hand over the wound, his bemused expression signifying the problem of coming to terms with his loss. And Peter, by now having had second thoughts, points aimlessly at what he has done and appeals to the fleeing St Mark. A soldier sets off in pursuit, either to arrest the fugitive or hand back the shirt the Evangelist has left in his charge. The comic nature of this is pointed by the amazed soldiers leaning against the balustrade, looking down on Peter's precipitate act.

The chill of the classical terrace offsets the full-blooded action going on under its imposing proportions. Here and there on the terrace the other disciples have scattered to various points behind the balustrade. Other spectators have also gathered to overlook the dramatic events. Soon they are themselves to be overlooked on Golgotha. The sublime themes of Crucifixion and Judgement are dominant in a sky streaked with red. Christ's blood, indeed, 'streams in the firmament'[10].

It is the twofold vision again which evokes our complex response to this picture – one of Carel Weight's major works.

When he deals with the dignified and sublime he is on his guard as, indeed, Bruegel was before him. 'Some untidy spot' of a run-down suburb will do for his *Woman Taken in Adultery* (1955) – it will strike the note of truth. It is an old lesson in which he is deeply learned and repeats with novel variations. For instance, in this picture we have a sleazy corner with a slatted bench on which a man sits scrawling something in the dust with his stick. An ugly alleyway leads to the main road – in it three individuals have their backs to us. A cyclist passes and looks back over his shoulder – at what? A woman staggering away from a bearded chap on the bench. No more. It happens all the time – a man giving his wife a good dressing down.

We are, by such means, 'locked into the situation', as Mervyn Levy has said. Nor is there anything didactic here. It is representation, purely. We may be as indifferent as the three in the alley and turn our backs, or look away as the cyclist must as he hurries off.

**Crucifixion (1959)**
*Oil on panel, 96 × 60in (243.8 × 152.4cm),*
*Harris Museum and Art Gallery, Preston,*
*Lancashire.*

It is a power of arrest difficult to resist, this appeal to the spectator to participate – and his work was 'catching on'. As you wandered round the numerous 'shows' and exhibitions you would catch the air of excitement – always Weight-engendered – and hear such preferences urged as: 'If I had any choice in the matter – I'd come away with Weight's *Betrayal*.' Or you might overhear someone snapping an intrusive friend into silence: 'Yes – do you mind? I'm interested in all those people gawping at Calvary.' Or, in a small private gallery mounting a one-man show, more likely than not there'd be well-off wives pressing their husbands to buy anything quirky, or even a sombre, almost depressing river nocturne because: 'Weight's so good at the "creeps".'

He'd been brought before the public in a television feature – along with his friend Ruskin Spear – in 1958. His prices were modest, and his pictures were bought steadily by the less well-off and at breakneck speed by the more affluent – especially the 'creepy' subjects, which sold like hot cakes. He 'grabs' us, as the Americans say, with all the dramatic, often melodramatic, devices at his command.

The same power can be exercised more subtly, allowing us freedom to look around and search for what it is that arouses our curiosity. It's up to us to feel curious enough to push our way into the press of working people to make sure that Christ sits side-saddle on the donkey, or on the edge of the little cart. But the great concourse accompanying home, as it were, their 'Man-of-the-Match' under the decorations supplied by the authorities, cannot leave us outsiders for long. But it's not all that homespun. True, it does look like a northern mining town, but besides the bunting there's a real angel floating over the roof of a terrace perched high on the upper levels. And there's a trumpet to his mouth, for it is nothing less than *Christ's Entry into Jerusalem* (1958, page 50).

Not only is there the truth of down-to-earth realism, elevated by some mysterious, mystical presence (and we can make of that what we will), there is the excitement of the subject matter and the sheer joy of the painting as powerful pieces in Weight's artistic armoury. There is much for us to look for, and much for us to question.

Is it humility that leads Carel Weight to approach his *Crucifixion* (1959, page 51) from some remote point behind Calvary? Is it to avoid heroics and the traditional? Is William Blake's *Crucifixion* of 1800 (Fitzwilliam Museum, Cambridge) a decisive influence? These are possibilities. 'The Way I Work' gives insight into the process of the subject 'taking him over', achieving a vital aspect of the composition as if of itself – the 'magic hand of chance' taking control (see page 14, note 16 and page 15, note 20).

The curious hand-shaped block of Golgotha – to Helen Roeder it was like a sombre, cavernous pyx – holds the three crosses in poise against the triangular mass of people, and guides our attention to the apex, to the background shrubbery, the trees and fiery sky. From our remote viewpoint we see only the arms of the crucified pinned to the crossbeam. The spectators – attitudes sharply defined – display concern, curiosity, indifference. The central cross holds the mocking inscription into a lowering scud of red cloud. Higher than its two fellows, receiving the strong illumination from a rift in the clouds, it dominates the scene, a magnificent image sprung from profound spiritual soundings.

But humanity is Weight's dominant interest, and this rearward, elevated approach allows him to concentrate on the spectators, whose reactions convey the significance of the event.

# 5

## SURREALISM AND THE CONVERSATION PIECE
### River and Sea Pictures – Portraits and Genre
### (The 1950s)

———————————————— • ————————————————

In *The Artist* magazine, November 1988, Jane Stroud wrote that Carel Weight, 'strongly influenced by Surrealism. . . found the excitement of the imagination akin to his natural artistic instincts'.

Surrealist material comes as much through the illogic of conscious thought as through the irrationality of the dream – through, in fact, the waking-dream, the visionary faculty. Carel Weight told me that his weirdest, wildest of river scenes in *Land of the Birds* (1987–88, page 122) was suggested by his seeing 'a few marks on a piece of paper'. Then he added, almost under his breath: 'It's rather a strange thing going on there, isn't it?' The remark was as applicable to the queer picture as to the process which produced it – via a string of mental activities closely akin to the surrealist, automatic process.

Obsessions, gristing from childhood in the subconscious, influenced the way Weight looked at things. One night he observed, through a partly curtained, lighted window, a solitary man sitting against the farther wall. He sat with his hands pinioned together, while a figure – as if from another world – glided darkly by, unheeding and detached. Excited by such promptings, Weight's imagination created the phantasms of his surrealism. This particular experience produced the cell-like interior of *Despair* (1969, page 81).

Closely in touch with reality, he finds his chimera in ordinary, matter-of-fact circumstances; and subjects, avowedly dream-engendered, are rooted in the actual – *The Dream*, *The Invasion*, for example, and especially the *Medusa* pictures (pages 79 and 111), and even the 'innocent' *Dream about a Flower* (page 26). We should recall his response to Norman Rosenthal's suggestion that he might have shown 'with the surrealist groups in London.' Weight was aware of the possibility. He had, in fact, helped to 'organise a surrealist exhibition before the war.' 'But I didn't feel that my particular brand of surrealism was quite the sort of fashionable, popular idea about it really.'[1] Weight's images may be those of nightmare, logic may be stretched and strained, but it is never set at naught. Perhaps that is what he meant – that his 'brand of surrealism' was too open to an immediate, commonsense interpretation.

Referring to this particular field, Weight said:

> I admired de Chirico – he was one of my first heroes. His silences, brooding skies and immense distances impressed me tremendously.

*A Walk with Camille Pissarro* (page 94) has something of these qualities and a de Chirico-like oppressiveness invades the idyllic *The Song of the Bird* (page 98). Deep silences reign over the street outside *The Friends'* sitting room (page 85) and in the gardens of *Sunshine and Shadow* and of *The Silence* itself (page 83).

Weight's second surrealist hero was Salvador Dalí, whose clear expression and psychological probings he found most impressive. And Weight, in a rare exploitation of Dalí's manipulative skill, so arranges two of the *grilli* in *Thoughts of the Girls* (page 82) that they create the illusion of double figuration – of two separate images existing simultaneously in the same figure. But that is an isolated example, and on the whole, Weight's 'brand of surrealism' did not conform to the 'fashionable, popular idea'.

A servant addresses her mistress: *'He put Her in an Acid-Bath, Miss'* (1949). The title is a bit of wayward fun, which did in fact, backfire. We must think of this conversation piece as a superb travesty of Vermeer whose calm, ordered science does not escape – attracts rather – the inconsequential experiments of Salvador Dalí. And a surrealist ghost hovers, does it not, somewhere in the maladroit association between the conversation piece and its title, *'He put Her in an Acid-Bath. . .'*?

Bella provided the material. Described by Helen Roeder as more family retainer than servant, she was taken on by Miss Roeder and Carel Weight following the death of Miss Roeder's mother. She spoke in a heavily

**Interior (1949)**
*Oil on canvas, 48 × 38in (121.9 × 96.5cm),*
*Royal West of England Academy, Bristol.*

**As I wend to the shores I know not, As I list to the dirge, the voices of men and women wreck'd (1951)**
*Oil on panel, 48 × 120in (121.9 × 304.8cm), Oldham Art Gallery.*

accented Wicklow dialect, with the aggrieved undertone characteristic of the speech of the true Dubliner. Her often lugubrious repertoire was transmuted into pure gold by the extravaganza of her rhetoric.

But *'He put Her in an Acid-Bath, Miss'* did not redound to Weight's advantage. 'It failed to sell,' he said, 'so I changed the title to *Conversation Piece* and it sold at once.'

The conversation piece was a frequent exercise. *Interior* (1949, page 53) – as the original acid-bath announcement came to be known – was a return to the comfortable intimacy of *The Sewing Machine* (1938). A lady, seated at the breakfast table, has turned her chair the better to indulge her domestic help, who has yet to clear the table and stands, arms folded, expecting a good chatty exchange. The objects on the table – china, and plant in earthenware pot – the room furnishings, are lovingly precise in definition.

Weight returned to the river for the idyll of *Teddington Lock* (1950, page 19), a study which has been discussed earlier (see page 18) and the London parks were benign in service to his art. Sydenham was bountiful. In *Holland Walk* (*c*.1946, page 45), he indulged the sense of freedom in the spring following the war; here, too, *The Strange Bird* (*c*.1952) perched close to delight him with its beauty. The Shakespearean upsurge, under Laurence Olivier's authority, was recognised in Chiswick Park (*The Ghost of Pyramus and Thisbe* (*c*.1950), and later the frieze-like *Midsummer Night's Dream*), while the fag-end of a day, burning down behind the trees in Bishop's Park, crystallised all its drama in the sad, unnoticed *Presence* (1955, page 110).

Turner ranks among the foremost of Weight's heroes. Turner's sea pictures, with their resonant music, awakened deep responses in him.

His was a musical family. His mother was 'passionately fond of music',[2] and his father could elicit a tune from any instrument that came to hand. Carel Weight himself was every bit as 'musical', and had 'a powerful baritone voice which his parents decided should be trained'. But the lessons quickly lapsed, owing to the drastic teaching methods of his tutor. She was, he told Mervyn Levy

> an enormously fat lady who used to lay me on the carpet – I was about sixteen at the time – then pile volumes of the *Encyclopaedia Britannica* on my chest and make me sing my scales. Sometimes she used to sit on my stomach! So I began to dislike singing. I went to my parents and said, 'I really *can't* do this sort of thing. I haven't got the physique.'

His passion for music was, however, undiminished – proved at every stage of his life, and particularly during the war in his pursuit of operas and concerts even when rushed off his feet by assignments in Italy and Austria. Carel Weight's music is all his own. There are, for instance, the quietudes of *The Silence* (1965, page 83) and *Fallen Woman* (1967, page 86), the minor chords of *The Battersea Park Tragedy* (1974, page 92) and the

Orovida was a very sweet and wonderful person. . . Rather than trying to hide or disguise [her fatness] she did everything she could to make it more obvious – such as wearing brilliant colours with obvious decorative motifs that focused attention upon her girth. And strangely, instead of making her grotesque, this sort of attire made her *magnificent*.

The words are more exactly in keeping with the later portrait in the Ashmolean at Oxford. Oddly enough, Weight is somewhat dismissive of this. Further on in the above extract, 'There is another version in the Ashmolean,' is all he says. In the first picture he views Orovida from an elevated point which exaggerates the lady's obesity, compresses her features, narrows her eyes and renders the face smoothly, inscrutably oriental. This was the painter's purpose – to allow the sitter to reflect her devotion to eastern, particularly Chinese, *objets d'art*.

We might find the work disconcerting. It disturbs, but that, surely, was the very response Carel Weight was after. So if we try to establish a preference for the second, more traditional picture, we risk quarrelling with the artist's set intention in painting the first. The preference rests with the individual observer.

In the later version (1957, page 58) he observes her on the level of her chair, looking directly into her face. This is carefully modelled and the fine, steady eyes speak of the character he has described so warmly. We can sense Orovida's weight under her boldly striped dress, the breathing life of the large body so fully in occupation of the chair. The face reveals the contented acceptance of which the painter has spoken, the robust intelligence, patience and generous tolerance.

In his later portraiture Weight often favours the angled floor to thrust the subject peremptorily on the attention, or to stress some feature relevant to the sitter's character or situation. In *Miss Hursey* (c.1952) the high-level viewpoint opens up the restricted area of the room to emphasise the woman's isolation. The carpet is angled sharply under her feet and the chair tilts her forward. Again, other angled pieces of furniture are ranged starkly against the wall. These chilly arrangements exaggerate the uneasiness of Miss Hursey, who is elderly and looks tense. Her clumsy hands, veins ridged and enlarged, are placed firmly on either knee and seem troublesome and exposed. *Miss Hursey* and Rembrandt's *Old Woman Seated* (1654) share the kinship of having been summoned from habitual self-effacement to an unwanted prominence. They would withdraw from the sharp scrutiny if they could, but they provoke thoughts on the human predicament too rich for the artist to forego. 'The eye listens,' as Paul Claudel says – in these portraits hearing the 'still sad music of humanity.'[7]

I like all the bits and pieces to relate to the sitter in a very intimate way. They are a vital extension of the life of the subject.[8]

In the very early portrait of *Rose* (1929, page 8) a simple yellow flower and a plain mahogany sideboard were the emblems of a tender and firm-hearted loyalty. Nine years later, with the portraits of Edna (pages 26 and 27) these devices become more numerous and complex. These were indeed 'vital extensions', which have to be distinguished from other inclusions of a narrative element chosen also to have a cogent bearing on the character of the sitter. An early example is *The Visitor* (1952), a prize-winning picture Weight painted at the time he was working on *Miss Hursey*.

It is an uncomfortable portrait of old age. The poor soul fronts us in her chair, 'darkling' as Whistler's famous *Mother*. She sits, exposed and unprotected, as the Skeleton Summoner appears in a glass panel of the open door. Nor can she turn to face her visitor, but sits heavily in her chair, held down by the weight of her black lace-up boots. Mervyn Levy remarks on the alien nature of the furniture. The china cabinet is set back at the furthest remove, with doors that have a dead, unopened look.

Levy observes that 'the hands are crossed uncertainly. The feet seem to say, "This is not my carpet."' Indeed not, as the carpet shelves from under her feet, lifts and then climbs towards the skirting. A disconcerting composition, owing as much to the austerity of its lines and angles as to its stage management.

A hard life has corrugated the frail hands with veins, its rigours are etched in lines about the eyes and mouth. It is deeply despondent, for whatever may once have claimed the poor soul's affection, is now as aloof and cold as the china in the closed cupboard. The only substantial claim on her attention is the inevitable, insubstantial skeleton (*The Visitor*).

**Orovida Pissarro (1956)**
*Oil on canvas, 36 × 28in (91.4 × 71.1cm),*
*Tate Gallery, London.*

**Orovida Pissarro II (1957)**
*Oil on canvas, 36 × 28in (91.4 × 71.1cm),*
*Ashmolean Museum, Oxford.*

Narrative painting also occupied Weight, particularly in the later half of this first post-war decade. Of these works, *The Presence* (1955, page 110) is the finest. On one occasion Carel Weight and I had the room and the picture to ourselves. It was a rare moment, when genius felt that it could lower its guard. I had commented – as I judged, appropriately – on the superb sunset in the picture, and he laughed quietly with a warmth stimulated by the recollection of past triumph. More than one critic, he told me, had commended it as one of the finest sunsets since Turner. Then he resumed the guard: 'But it's not for me to say that!'

I questioned him on the origin of these pictures, which for all the world look so very like observations of everyday life. But, 'No – they're purely imaginary.' Even so, they could reproduce reality. Half-way up Keswick Road, East Putney, at its corner with Portinscale Road, a confusion of priorities invites accidents (*Dangerous Corner c.* 1956, page 13). But – as far as Weight knew – no pavement artist had ever set up his exhibits against *The Yellow Wall* (1951, page 60). Only in his mind's eye had he observed a nightwatchman's interest in a squabbling family going home from Ravenscourt Park Station (*The Active and the Contemplative Life* 1955, page 64). He was in his element with these subjects, which provided ample scope for that dynamism he has made his speciality.

In *With Uncle Joe to Richmond* (1952, opposite), an idealised recollection of childhood, the boy Carel, seated on the carrier of his uncle's bike, looks up admiringly at his indulgent, favourite uncle. No doubt he questions him on their progress, and the riverside attractions to which they are steering.

They are crossing a bridge, impelled by the strong laterals of curb, pavement and balustrade which direct the flow of movement. Any harshness of line is softened by the river's graceful bend and the elegant, distant bridge with its ivory piers reflected in the water. Overhead the limpid sky is traced with thin, glowingly benign clouds.

A plump lady on the bridge moves towards us, but looks at the cyclists. Set in the first plane of the picture and cropped by the frame, her figure presses physically close – a device characteristic of these 'moving pictures'. A prim lady contributes additional movement, picking her way genteelly across the bridge. Sedately and soon, the cycle, under the upright pilotage of Uncle Joe, will pass her, and all this fluidity is crucially offset by the stationary figure of a man leaning over the parapet and looking down on the approaching steamer. It is a beautifully harmonised impression of a carefree, unpremeditated moment enjoyed on a gracious, leisurely day. An idyll certainly, whose vigorous, dynamic laterals eliminate anything like the sentimental, but the whole softened sufficiently to avoid anything too harsh on the eye.

'Uncle Joe' was, in fact, Weight's favourite uncle, Percy Williams. Like his sister, Carel's mother, he was a first-rate chiropodist, though he loathed the job and devoted time and energy to 'various inventions, none of which came to anything'. He designed and built model aeroplanes which he and Carel would fly on Wimbledon Common. He was venturous and gambled with little success, but the child Carel thought him wonderful. We will see him later as the stupendous conjuror in *The Masterstroke of Dr Tarbusch* (1960, page 120), an affectionate tribute to Uncle Percy's prowess in legerdemain. 'He had a way with him,' says Carel Weight.

*The Yellow Wall* (1951) was for Weight a local and a lucky feature – more than a found object, rather a *local trouvé* – which served his concept perfectly. It is built in a series of panels, decorated by a sequence of oblong patterns in blue bricks and linked end-to-end by cross-over lacings in blue headers. The device may be a crudely opened-out version of an arabesque, as may be seen in the Sala del Reposo and elsewhere in the Alhambra. Static and moving elements are of equal importance in the composition. Each element offsets the other, while the 'arabesque' devices run the eye to-and-fro across the wall, the separate panels enforcing a 'rest' when the static element so demands. The wall serves, therefore, as a 'tensioning rail' between the opposing interests – the poor, dead-beat pavement artist sitting alongside his exhibits, and the cyclists pedalling strenuously home.

How finely Weight disperses human interest – between the self-centred cyclists and the charitable patron of art. Or is it a more rigorous situation, with the artist being 'moved on'? Behind the wall, other 'characters' – the trees – interpose with their presage of a coming storm, and bluster against an overcast sky – every reason the cyclists should pedal hard; even more urgent that the artist should effect a sale to afford his lodging for the night.

He sits with cupped hand and face raised appealingly to the man who, we trust, will make an offer. With him we have looked at the works for sale – a clumsy display encompassing larger-than-life subjects: an elephant, an outsize dog with walking-stick in muzzle and labelled 'Man's Friend', a portrait of Stalin, a flag

**With Uncle Joe to Richmond (1952)**
*Oil on board, 27 × 15in (68.5 × 38cm),*
*Sotheby's, London.*

of empire with lion's head superimposed, and, as climax, a toy galleon on a pond with immense ducks in the foreground. It is the simple entertainment of a morality, making its point with all the emphasis of the commonplace.

Four years later, the yellow wall again asserts those opposites of flight and arrest. Carel Weight's account of *The Moment* (1955, page 61) somewhat resembles Munch's well-known explanation of *The Scream* (1893):

> I thought of a scream – a scream from the hurrying figure in the foreground. And then
> – something awful – perhaps she is just about to be killed by a car or a bus – or has
> already been killed – and the scream is all that remains. This is the moment of truth.[9]

Again, the wall gives its strong thrust to the rushing figure. Further up along the road someone has been halted in his tracks, frozen by what is about to happen. The frail, flurried girl offers ineffectual resistance with her left hand feebly, involuntarily raised. Her gesture, terrified look and scream are all directed at the viewer to engage him in the action. Again, behind the wall, are other observers – trees, like the onlooker higher up the road, rooted and agitated. Spruce-like growths spread a dark fan above the sheets of corrugated metal which round off the wall near the turning into Buttermere Drive. A cedar broods, impassively watchful. Deciduous branches, cuffed by a freshening gust, wave, or thrash against the flushed sky.

The subject is as much concerned with sound as with precipitate flight. The rough arabesques of the yellow wall rush down the road in ascending scale, pushing the girl headlong to the concluding dissonance of the corrugated screen.

The painter has known this part of East Putney over many years. It is as familiar to him as his own garden which he found 'an unending source of inspiration. I have imagined all sorts of wonders there.'[10] Keswick Road was almost equally fecund, productive of so much drama against its yellow wall – a solid enough structure, but embodying for the visionary those vital contraries without which there is no progression.

*Cops and Robbers* (1956, page 62) may be judged to be uncomfortably close to illustration. The earlier *Going Home* (1950, page 63) provides a richer human interest and represents a familiar experience.

Two schoolchildren – a boy and a girl – cycle home and are about to negotiate the traffic outside East Putney Station. A cyclist pedals up briskly on his sports model following a staid-looking motorcyclist moving cautiously on to the carriageway. A box-shaped milk float, horse-drawn and plodding, gives impetus to the cyclists' speed. There is a general sense of urgency, as an overcast sky looks threatening with red patches of racing clouds. A few pedestrians in the station approach appear apprehensive. In spite of this, a man lingers. He has drawn his bike alongside the curb and, relaxing on the saddle, observes the children with an interest which can only be equivocal. *Going Home*, therefore, provides cause for concern – quite absent from *Cops and Robbers*, which concentrates solely on the physical issues of a straightforward drama of flight and pursuit.

**The Yellow Wall (1951)**
*Oil on canvas, 29 × 36in (73.6 × 91.4cm),*
*Barnfield Museum, Halifax.*

*Cops and Robbers* might well be omitted were it not for the curious story attaching to it. It would be wrong, even so, not to admire the sharp draughtsmanship, the tremendous contrast between the massive railway architecture and the slight figures of pursued and pursuers, or to note how the tapering and towering lines of masonry give such force to the movement. Understandably, Weight spoke appreciatively of the work. 'It was a good subject for me,' he said, and then he told his extraordinary story.

> Soon after the picture was sold the owner wrote to me wondering if I were at all clairvoyant. The picture, he said, reproduced an event – in fact, a turning point in his life. I didn't like to take the matter up, particularly if he were on the side of the youths being chased by the police! But some time later he wrote again to say that my picture had had such an enormous effect on him that he'd like to reproduce it, and could he have my permission. I answered that if he intended using it for commercial reasons I would have to charge him some fee for the copyright, but if not, if it were for some other purpose – for his family, for instance – then I'd make no objection. He wrote back to say that he was going to use it as an illustration to a text. Whether he was a religious 'Enthusiast', I've never discovered. . . But what a strange correspondence it was! Even now I've not fathomed what was in the picture to be so significant. Whether he's still got it, whether he's still alive, I don't know – it's many years ago. . . I'd like to see it again, but there – I don't suppose it's very likely.

A railway station – better still, the station approach where arrivals and departures can be studied more profitably, is a first-rate provisioner for the narrative artist. The flared funnelling-out lands us fair and square in the heart of the goings-on. That was so in *Going Home*, where the flanking walls of the high-level embankment open out and thrust the cyclists on to the thoroughfare.

The approach at Ravenscourt Park on the District Line is put to a similar, though quieter, purpose in *The Active and the Contemplative Life* (1955, page 64). Nor is movement in Weight always so extreme; in this picture it is more on the level of psychology. He avoids any obvious clash between the two conditions. No need for that. The contrary states are recognisable at once. Under-emphasis here suits the subject admirably, perhaps reflecting its New Testament origin. A more likely source is Rossetti's watercolour of Rachel and Leah in the *Purgatorio*.

**The Moment (1955)**
*Oil on panel, 24 × 72in (60.9 × 182.8cm),*
*Castle Museum, Nottingham.*

**Cops and Robbers (1956)**
*Oil on canvas, 36 × 48in (91.4 × 121.9cm),*
*private collection.*

The urban setting demands a fresh, entirely original interpretation. Any too classical, or over-romantic, visioning is controlled by the dour realities of the theatre of action. Old familiar themes present themselves ready-dressed and rehearsed in Carel Weight's contemporary theatre. Under ideal conditions, the areas, streets and parks of London, the modest gardens of suburbia, offer the subjects ready-made. A quiet look of reproach from a man on a corner bench suggests the *Woman taken in Adultery* (1955). A gesture of quite modest emphasis, if exaggerated, could belong to some modern Tarquin raping his Lucretia in a back garden. A child halts, unaccountably rapt, on the footbridge of *Barnes Station* (1976, page 95), arrested by the vision of the Cross. And *The Battersea Park Tragedy* (1974, page 92) only awaited his visit before springing at once into visionary existence.

We should regard a station approach as symbolic of flux and instability. A nightwatchman sits over his fire and a little family group makes its way home. Such familiar circumstances favour – enforce – Carel Weight's simplest language.

The celebrant of the commonplace, he is acutely aware of the excitements which underlie the surface. They rise to the surface here in the station approach, doubtless to break out fully once the family gets home. Father shies from the wife's remonstrance – he's heard it all before, and the children, neutral in their own worlds, follow resignedly. The youngest sulks, refusing the proffered hand of her elder sister. The boy hangs back, wholly unco-operative.

**Going Home (1950)**
*Oil on canvas, 36 × 60in (91.4 × 152.4cm),*
*private collection / Sotheby's, London.*

It is an oft-repeated act in the human tragi-comedy where we, in the 'active life', assume these leading roles at one time or another. Returning home with the family at the fag-end of a weary day is following an all too familiar script.

To the right sits the nightwatchman, more than likely 'free from the entanglements of married life. . . to have leisure and peace for contemplation.'[11] He looks into the fire, pondering his assessment of the active life.

The setting is soberly toned. A melancholy blueness overspreads the scene, intensified by the single black spruce standing over the nightwatchman's hut. The brazier emits drifts of blue smoke.

The Wordsworthian in Weight chooses humble life where 'the essential passions of the heart. . . are less under restraint and speak a plainer and more emphatic language'.[12]

Thus the station approach mounts a comic juxtaposition of the troubled and the tranquil. Weight allows himself a lighthearted comment on the merits of the two states. The nightwatchman's coals glow with steady warmth, and the little dog stands squarely, no doubt sagaciously, on the contemplative side.

It is a human show whose truth induces us to take thought. The melancholy blue suggests a wistfulness, a regret that things aren't rather different. We may see the nightwatchman's thread of blue smoke as a cord attaching him to the others – the 'finite hearts that yearn'.

Again, that could be an over-serious assessment. Indeed, thoughtfulness will be part of the entertainment, and the lightness of touch invites us to smile. That should be a suitable response – as long as the smile is charitable.

The charm of life opposes the cold of *The Dark Tower* (1957, page 64), a stark image in the Gothic tradition of Browning's ultimate mausoleum.[13] But in the very heart of the picture, flowers in three bouquets shine in their tissue wrappings against the hulking masonry of the wall, used – as previously – as the common denominator to the clearly individualised interests. Not unlike the wall in Giotto's famous *Pietà*, this urban barrier ties the actors together in their own areas of personal significance. Behind the wall, to which road and pavement run parallel, looms the Dark Tower. Just now the road is clear of traffic; it could be a Sunday afternoon scene and, once again, we are invited to assist in the action by the close approach of the figures cropped by the lower frame.

**The Active and the Contemplative Life (1955)**
*Oil on canvas, 40 × 55in (101.6 × 139.7cm), Reading Museum and Art Gallery.*

A moribund growth has stretched thin stems above the wall, but however forbidding the associations, a quiet interlude is in play on the pavement and street. A dog is being walked by his slim mistress. On the opposite pavement a young girl, with a flair for style, is dressed attractively for her escort – whom we only partly see, as both are well on their way out of the picture. Once more, the urban theatre brings a restraint to bear upon any strong tendency towards the romantic. 'Life is real. Life is earnest.' You feel the three bouquets proffered to the young people, centre stage, are items of commerce rather than romance. Behind these, a young man turns as if to speak to the lady with the dog. For one brief moment the stylishly dressed girl looks round to observe our interest in what these suspended acts will come to. Will the flowers be bought, or rejected? Will the man and young woman exchange words, or will the dog, straining at his leash, pull his mistress away? Will humanity challenge the residual cold of the Dark Tower? For what other reason are the flowers so prominent if not to affirm the supremacy of life and love?

It was a prolific decade. Promptings came powerfully to Carel Weight, and a joyous expenditure of energy, directed as freedom chose, accounted for some of his finest work.

**The Dark Tower (1957)**
*Oil on panel, 48 × 36in (121.9 × 91.4cm), private collection.*

# 6

# THROUGH THE SIXTIES I
## Religious Themes

———————————— • ————————————

'Religion in itself isn't that important to me, but it provides one with wonderful themes.' Carel Weight was speaking to Norman Rosenthal in 1981 in the interview[1] referred to previously.

It is difficult to regard the sixties as remarkable for any upsurge of religious enthusiasm. In fact, there is a strong whiff of the period – the 'Swinging Sixties' – blowing through Weight's work. Nor should we assume that the great *Crucifixion* of 1959 engendered a momentum in religious feeling which, beginning with *The Road to Calvary* (1960, page 66) continued right through to the Bible pictures of 1968. He was always open to scriptural hints and whispers. It just so happened that both Manchester and Oxford commissioned large religious undertakings and consequently increased his usual output of such work during the period.

A holiday in Brittany gave him *The Road to Calvary*. He was met in Dieppe by his friend, Alistair Grant – later to be a fellow contributor to *The Oxford Illustrated Old Testament* – and from there they drove the great distance to Auray 'in Grant's luxurious car'. (Carel Weight has never driven: no surprise when we recall his service in the Royal Armoured Corps, from which he was soon transferred as – to report Helen Roeder – 'it was patently obvious that Carel driving a tank would be a danger to the supporting troops'.[2]) At one of the many stops *en route* he sketched a typical Breton church, which later was to overlook his *Road to Calvary*.

He did not treat the subject in the exaggerated forms of Spencer's version, for Spencer's vocabulary required exaggeration to communicate the mystical impact of the event on Cookham. Such was not Weight's intention. But where naturalism is at all strained – as in the queer faces and gestures of the spectators on the walls – it is to establish the excited atmosphere and index the emotions and attitudes the occasion stimulates.

A crowd has poured on to the village street to witness the scene and enjoy the fine spring afternoon. For some, it disrupts the routine of an ordinary day. A man is in his working clothes. A woman, dressed for some happier occasion, finds this more absorbing. Children quarrel, indifferent to what is happening. For most, it is an unexpected diversion, and not to be missed.

It is not easy to spot the leading characters of the drama. The earnest-looking man, pressing forward a little in advance of the troops, could be the 'man from Cyrene'. But the three Holy Women are lost in the crowd. Perhaps two have just come into the picture at the left, and strain urgently forward. Is the Virgin the girl with the Alice-band, walking close to the dragging base of the cross?

The church – aloof from the suffering, indifference and wrongful purpose – points skyward, duly noting the time.

And time is a problem for the nervous girl, sitting tense in Carel Weight's garden. How can she possibly get through this sitting in her state of nerves? In a momentary gleam, the artist sees her agitation as the concern of the Annunciate Virgin, 'troubled at the Angel's saying'. It is

> the intersection of the timeless
> With time.[3]

Such an epic moment: which Weight's alchemy renders down to something acceptable – a jittery girl in a garden chair!

But what a strange, eponymous *Departing Angel* (1961, page 67)! Pope reliably(?) informs us that

> Spirits, freed from mortal laws, with ease
> Assume what sexes and what shapes they please.[4]

Which may be so, but St Matthew's Angel is unquestionably male. Carel Weight's is determinedly female, even to woolly jumper and comfy house shoes.

As she walks away she examines her fingers, reflecting deeply. Why? In my youth I would see my mother

**The Road to Calvary (1960)**
*Oil on board, 67 × 102in (170 × 260cm),*
*Simon Langton Grammar School,*
*Canterbury.*

examine her fingers like this when they were arthritic. But that won't do! Perhaps she takes tally of the assignments that await attention, or marks off those already discharged. No awe-inspiring Gabriel, this, but a poor wraith-like creature with little of the celestial about her. She retreats across the chilly flagstones, raising ashen-grey hands to ashen-grey face.

Nothing wraith-like about the girl. She stays plumply put in the garden chair, her pleated skirt spread fanwise above knees and fine legs, court shoes showing off to advantage her slim ankles. Her chic abbreviations – the antithesis of the Angel's dowdy gear – might allude to the permissiveness inaugurated by the sixties. *Thoughts of the Girls* (1967, page 82) will make similar references.

If the title did not insist upon the Annunciation, we might assume that here was a guardian angel (there are several in Weight's *oeuvre*) deserting its charge. That was always a possibility! We could then approach the picture from a secular standpoint, when questions would arise closely related to an approach approved by divinity. In any case, Carel Weight has not been rigidly orthodox.

For instance: why such a sulky expression on the face of the young woman? What is the symbolic purpose of the stone lion *couchant*? Does it make a sardonic comment on the sensibilities of the wayward flesh? Is the Angel an embodiment of the girl's thoughts? Is this her *alter ego* in later life?

I boldly outlined a few of these ideas.

'When you're working,' he said, 'a lot of things may occur to you subconsciously. But I wanted to throw emphasis, not on the Angel or her tidings, but rather on the feelings directly afterwards. The Angel's had her say, and the other's got to make the best of it.'

I ventured my approval of the Angel's comfy-looking house-shoes. The painter agreed. 'They've a good way to go. I expect they'd have to be fairly comfortable!'

Serious discussion was suspended.

The idea for *Day of Judgement* (1961) occurred to him as he sketched a spacious garden overlooked by his

**Departing Angel (1961)**
*Oil on canvas, 36 × 36in (91.4 × 91.4cm),*
*Royal Academy of Arts Collection.*

Chelsea studio. A garden-fête setting, he decided, would suit the sublime theme very well. In that way he could 'bring it down to earth', and express it in characteristically familiar terms. In the event the terms were uneasy.

We must regard the leading, abnormally agitated characters as Spiritual Forms, such as we see in El Greco, William Blake and Stanley Spencer, changed 'in the twinkling of an eye' from their old physical selves. Now, as Souls of the Righteous, who have passed the Great Adjudication, they abandon themselves to the Dance of Eternal Delight in Paradise. Later, in 1973, the subject is more fully developed as *The Last Judgement*.

*Day of Doom* (page 69) was begun the following year (1962), and was in his studio for the next ten years, during which period it underwent numerous adjustments and revisions. The dramatic effects, right dispositions of the characters; the patterns, balance, colours and movement were the ingredients of a particularly complex composition. The concept developed out of the general, communal fear of the atom bomb, and the opening of the *Sequentia* of the Requiem Mass,

> *Dies irae, dies illa*
> *Solvet saeclum in favilla*

furnished the imagination of Carel Weight with a frightening scene from childhood.

A fire had broken out in a timber yard, threatening Rose's flat and the adjoining houses. The scene is a corner on Dawes Road, Fulham, which he knows like the back of his hand. The scene is brought to life with all the immediacy and intensity of a sensitive child's imagining. The bricks, flags and curbstones are meticulously in

67

place; the sign-written name on Messrs Batchelors' facia, the 'H' sign on the wall, the moulded panel under the window are as exact in their placing and as vivid as ever they were in childhood. So too the notices in the rags and bones shop, part of the long terrace immediately doomed. 'Everyone was very frightened and myself in particular when [I overheard a woman in the street saying], "If the wind changes all our houses will be burned down."'[5]

As if the child's imagination is directly tapped, the work is executed in solid, elemental forms.

The poor tenants stare in desperate astonishment from upstairs windows towards the source of some catastrophe outside the picture on the right. The dealer in rags and bones, living over the shop, leans out and is horrorstruck by what he sees. He covers his eyes, but cannot withdraw them from the fearful fascination. Clutching his forehead with a large protecting hand, he abandons himself to despair.

In the street the fugitives, confused and divided in their minds, make for safety in ways which panic determines.

Viewed from Batchelors' shop, the unfashionable terrace runs in a strong line towards the unseen terror. A crenellated frieze leaps up, across and down the frames of doors and windows and suggests instability, hurry and hysteria – leitmotifs of the work. We look through the shop windows – empty of goods against the 'great and terrible day' – at the cyclist pedalling in frenzied haste out, but in the direction which holds such fear for the onlookers at the windows. In her summery clothes and pretty hat – still in the pride of dress sense – she scurries along under cosmic fires. A frail, almost comic figure, she might symbolise the whole condition of man in the Ultimate Crisis.

As in the Book of Genesis, sublimity of thought is accommodated in a language void of decoration, so this 'Apocalypse of the Common Man' is conveyed in the simple linearity of Carel Weight's composition.

He laid aside his brush to allow time to point the further steps towards the completion of *Day of Doom*.

Honours now came to Carel Weight – the CBE in 1962 and election to the Royal Academy three years later. To Weight, honours are important in so far as they recognise the significance of art itself, not for what they may confer on the recipient. Alas, these distinctions did little to offset the near-anarchic conditions overshadowing his teaching life.

But the Academy laid claim to his unrivalled knowledge of Lowry and Spencer, saddling him with responsibilities he was delighted to accept. Sir Hugh Casson, President of the Royal Academy, wrote of Carel Weight's 'passionate interest in Spencer's work. . . so evident in his own painting'.[6] That influence was easy enough to spot in, for example, *The Return of the Prodigal Son* (1947, page 48), and in other religious work he adopts something of the exaggeration Spencer uses to convey spiritual fervour and the sense of the mystical. However, this idiom of exaggeration, in Weight's hands, produces such dramatic effects as Spencer himself would be proud to acknowledge. With Carel Weight, there is a control which the older master sometimes flouts to excess.

In the closing paragraph of the previous chapter, the phrase 'directed as freedom chose' might suggest that Weight's creative powers were at their full only when liberated from constraint, and that anything commissioned could be irksome. Mervyn Levy will tell us that 'he was not greatly interested in the commissioned portrait'.[7] But, on the whole, he enjoyed the challenge of providing something which satisfied the expectations of a patron. Of course, the subject had to be right.

'I have turned down painting the House of Lords in session,' he told Norman Rosenthal. 'I thought it was an absolutely unpaintable subject. I wouldn't know how to do it, it would be terrible.'[8]

But he welcomed commissions for religious work. And, difficult though it was to fit designs into the irregularities of the panels in the cut stone – a carpenter's job really – he thoroughly enjoyed working on the mural for Manchester Cathedral.

'I had a lot of difficulties. I found that every one of those little panels was a different size. Some were as much as two inches out. Bits had to be carved off here and there, and it was rather difficult.'

The first designs were done 'fairly quickly'. Indeed, the vigorously 'rushed' lines of the upper part of the mural – *Jesus and the People* – suggest the excess of excitement under which the initial concept was carried out in *Jesus and the People* at Harefield (see page 56).

The entire mural (1963, page 70) is enclosed in a mullioned Tudor arch cut into the south wall. It might originally have been intended for stained glass. It is, however, entirely without openwork, and Weight's designs fill the spaces instead. At the base, in a predella of small trefoiled panels, all but one of the *Beatitudes* are shown. Strikingly original, they exploit a range of dramatic effects characteristically his.

**(Opposite)**
**Day of Doom (1962–72)**
*Oil on panel, 60 × 55in (152.4 × 139.7cm),*
*Jeffrey and Catherine Horwood collection /*
*Royal Academy of Arts Library.*

**Jesus and the People and the Beatitudes (1963)**
*Oil on mural panels, Courtesy of the Dean and Canons of Manchester Cathedral.*

The central panel represents the *Pure in Heart* (all are captioned), and shows a male nude reaching heavenwards in ecstasy. A stream of white light floods down upon him. The concept is similar to Blake's *Dance of Albion*, commonly known as *Glad Day*. The gestures in both are expansive, but whereas Blake's figure displays a frontal nudity, Weight's, accommodated to the interior of an Anglican cathedral, is turned modestly the other way round.

In the panels which flank this single static figure, the Blessed Ones live out their principles in the world as it is. Full of colour and movement, they contrast with the central nude caught in the torrent of white light. The colour relations across the span of the predella are pretty obvious, and on that score there is no need for any tedious analysis. We see at once that brown associates with humility, purple with mourning, black with religious zeal.

Disregarding the Biblical order in the interests of composition, the sequence opens with *The Meek*. A delightful anachronism sets St Francis's Conversion of the Great Wolf of Agobio on the pavement above a London basement area. Clothed in the brown habit of his Order, he kneels on one knee and, backed by the area railings, receives the wolf's 'fealty'. Frightened faces appear in the basement windows. Other tenants crowd the small window on the ground floor, and lean out curious and alarmed. We are at that part of the *Fioretti* where the wolf promises Francis never again to prey on the citizens of Agobio.

> 'Friar Wolf, I desire that thou swear me fealty touching this promise, to the end that I may trust thee utterly.' Then St Francis held forth his hand to receive this fealty, and the wolf lifted up his right fore-paw and put it with friendly confidence in the hand of St Francis.[9]

This is exactly what we see, brought charmingly up to date, leaving us with the beguiling question: who is the exemplar of meekness – St Francis, or the Wolf? Of course, the answer is: both. A perfectly satisfactory answer.

*The Merciful* follows – another roadside scene, with the Samaritan's donkey looking on and ready to accept the burden of the Man who Fell Among Thieves. One of these – a mugger of today – is making off with his ill-gotten gains.

Next comes a violent domestic scene. The tiled floor and kitchen chair indicate an interior. *The Peacemaker* is grappling with the assailant, who has felled his victim with the chair. Later, by almost twenty years, the picture will be given broader treatment as one of the *Seven Deadly Sins* (1979–80, page 104).

Turning to the panels on the opposite flank, we see immediately next to the nude a young man who kneels in the roadside, one knee pressed tightly against the kerb. He is outside a branch of the Midland Bank, with his face averted from the house of commerce the better to concentrate on spiritual enrichment. Executives, men of affairs, a skilled manual worker – all pass him by without sparing a glance. In the modern sense of the phrase, this is what it means to *Hunger After Righteousness*.

There follows an episode in a poor, uncarpeted bedroom. On the cheap iron bed, his arm hanging limply to the floor, lies a young man. A woman – very possibly his wife – turns her back upon the bed in the anguish of bereavement. But in that famed eye-twinkling immediacy, her comfort is manifest in the hands that reach towards her across the bed.

Finally, a negro lad, walking to church, is abused by roughs who have waylaid him in the churchyard. They threaten violence, aim kicks at him, keeping themselves at a safe distance on the edge of the flagged path. Opposite, a great hand emerges; stigma-marked, it protects him, and urges him onward to the church door.

Weight follows the practice of the Masters of the old retables in unifying the several episodes with a feature common to all the panels of the predella. This is the hard chill of the stony foreground, an emblem well defining the mores of this world.

The two doors beneath the mural open into the chapter house, a newish annexe built upon mediaeval foundations. It dates from 1837, when the former parish church was raised to its cathedral status. Inside, and between the two door frames, is the small panel of *The Transfiguration and The Epileptic Boy*.

A stairway of broad steps, cut in the mountain overhang and railed for safety, curves sharply in its ascent to the summit. Here, in an outburst of light, Christ is transfigured. On the stairs the three Apostles stagger or hide their eyes. The 'bright cloud' of Matthew XVII floods down from the figure of Christ, then rushes in a torrent to the foot of the picture, where the healing of the boy takes place. He lies on a patch of green and the mist swirls about the onlookers. The mountain peak, with its great outcropping rocks, rides the mist like a craft seen in a nightmare. The precarious stairway, the insubstantial rocks, the substantial supporting mist, the curious juxtaposition of the two scenes, are as hallucinatory as the hauntings of the poor 'lunatick' boy. But the mist has thinned about the boy's head, over which Christ's hands are outstretched.

Three years later, 1966–7, another commission – this time from the Yorkshire side of the Pennines – reached Weight from the north. The civic authorities of Huddersfield asked him for a picture – either one of the town, or of some part of the surrounding landscape.

'I went out to Holmfirth, and my painting is a view of part of the town. I thought it was rather lovely, and I came back with enough material – certainly enough to paint this quite small picture.'

Initially entitled *The Serpent*, it was later renamed *The Garden of Eden*. Two people stand frozen and irresolute, startled by the appearance of a snake. A mature pair – the man is quite elderly – they confront the advancing creature. Their reaction affects us with a sense of physical shock and vulnerability. White-faced and trembling, the ageing hero snuggles his girl, as much for his own defence as for her protection. The half-smoked cigarette in his loose hand points feebly to the serpent's head; the woman's hands stretch stiffly down in a frail shield across their bodies. In taut parallels to the bents and blades of wild grass, these hands are the illuminated points in the dynamics of recoil and shocked impotence.

A massy wall of grey Pennine stone converges with the farther outhouse to define the apex of the menaced bower of this sorry version of Adam and Eve. Half-enclosed in the thick tangle of mixed growth, they stand entrapped. In front, long bents probe towards them; behind them, spear-grasses incline serpentine necks. A deep silence predominates, the dumbness of apprehension. But the sky and sweep of moorland, the angled and thinned-out firs, the bent grass waving, speak of a prevailing wind of perhaps sufficient strength to provide a music in perfect harmony with the subject.

There is another, a puzzling figure, seated and taking it easy a little further off. Who is this? There is no need to consult either the Bible or Milton for the identity. It is enough to respond to the vision as best we may within the scope of our sensibilities.

*The Oxford Illustrated Old Testament* was the idea of Edward Bawden, who was then a tutor in the Graphic School in Oxford. His plan was to have pictures – in pen-and-wash drawing – contributed by the best contemporary artists, most of whom were with him in the Graphic School. He and a panel of advisers chose

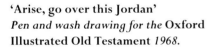

**'Arise, go over this Jordan'**
*Pen and wash drawing for the* **Oxford Illustrated Old Testament** *1968.*

the subjects they felt best suited to each individual talent, and assigned the responsibilities accordingly.

Weight might have felt that the historical Books of Joshua and 1 Kings implied the need to fall back upon his 'fine powers of recording', a reversion to exercises he had practised in the past. And perhaps there was some immediate diffidence in contemplating the task. In the Note he supplied at the back of each volume, he said that he found 'illustrating Isaiah more absorbing than a straightforward illustrative book like Joshua, for here one is on an uncharted sea where the artist sinks or swims on his own inner feelings'.

But he spoke to me of his reservation in rather stronger terms.

With prophecy, 'the vision of times afar off', he was released from historical record, and, in uniquely powerful idiom, could give the inspired pronouncements their contemporary relevance.

Even so, Joshua opened with a magnificently explosive design (above) to illustrate God's first command:

Arise, go over this Jordan, thou and all this people unto the land which I do give them.

A figure executed in starkly contrasting black and white, Joshua overlooks Jordan and the land beyond, above which the sun rises. Clouds in spread ink shape the image of God, his massive finger pointing to the heart of the sun. It is an epic concept, with Joshua on the heroic scale of Blake's Eternals.

Next, we are shown Joshua's spies hidden in the thatch of Rahab's house. Rahab stands in the entrance, misleading the King of Jericho's agents who have been sent to question her.

The costumes and the lightly constructed, single-floored house convey a sense of history. More subtly, this notion is given in the raised viewpoint from which we look down obliquely on the action and the spies just visible under the thatch.

Carel Weight depicted *The Fall of Jericho* with powerful economy. The rams' horns, in uplifted crescents, are answered by the inward-bending, collapsing masonry of the towers. An excessive and prolonged noise has been the great feature of Joshua's triumph. Again, the artist takes note of that capricious humour which, in life, may intrude upon the grand, or profoundly solemn, event. Jericho is not alone in suffering. One of Joshua's officers claps hands to his turban to muffle his ears and turns his anguished face towards us, as if to enlist our sympathy.

**But King Solomon Loved Many Strange
Women**
*Pen and wash drawing for the* **Oxford
Illustrated Old Testament** *1968.*

From 1 Kings he chose the dramatic episodes best suited to his art. Solomon, *Judging the disputed Motherhood*, raises an imperious hand to direct the halving of the child. The mother, with arms outflung, throws herself forward to restrain the servant who, with drawn sword, is ready to carry out the king's command. She pulls down the sword with so frenzied a grip that the man yells with pain.

In lesser hands the interpretation could have been overwrought and melodramatic. Indeed, monumentality was in order, with gestures strong enough to convey the emotion of the episode. Strength emanates from the splendid figure of Solomon. The mother's arms and flying hair, parallel to the drawn sword, are the basic lines which stress the deepest of all emotional pressures.

The next illustration shows *Solomon delivering his Proverbs and Songs* to all who have come from far and wide to hear him. He reaches out as if to seize illumination from the sun and clouds.

Other highly charged subjects – such as the wild landscape of *The Disobedient Prophet* (Chapter 13), *The Great Rain* (Chapter 15), the awesome fear of *The Stoning of Nabob* (Chapter 21) – are achieved through the simplest effects. Some, unfortunately, may be too reminiscent of John Martin and the religious epics of Hollywood. This stricture may be applicable to *Solomon and the Queen of Sheba* (Chapter 10), *Solomon Loved Many Strange Women* (Chapter 11, see above), the *Capture of Tirza* (Chapter 16) and Zedekiah's challenging the *Rival Prophet Micaiah* (Chapter 22). That Weight had given thought to the art of the film director is clear from the first sentence of his article, quoted earlier:

> The producer of the old silent film had to rely on gestures, the grouping, and the facial expressions of his actors to tell his story, but the illustrator, in addition, has to choose the frozen significant moment in time – he has but one shot.

**Thy daughters shall be carried upon their shoulders**
*Pen and wash drawing for the* **Oxford Illustrated Old Testament** *1968.*

I do not doubt for a moment that Carel Weight was well aware of the ludicrous lurking under the surface of these pompous episodes, and was deliberately dallying with the grand manners of Martin, Griffith and de Mille.

But the prophecy of Isaiah is beyond the reach of the ink-and-wash drawing, and Weight approached the task with his sturdy independence of mind. But at times his inventive energies flagged: illustrating the tremendous and the sublime has to be daunting – without the inhibiting triumphs of great forerunners in the background. In the article referred to above, having mentioned Giotto, Botticelli and Rembrandt, Carel Weight questions 'why the word "illustrative" is always used as a derogatory term by art critics'. He was certainly and fully aware of the demanding nature of his task.

Bawden and his advisers commissioned Carel Weight wisely, assigning to him that part of Isaiah where, after Chapter 38, a new voice is heard – the lofty Messianic prophecy of a later poetic genius.

Weight begins with the passage prophetic of the ministry of the Baptist, the opening of Chapter 40. A forbidding chain of hills runs across the design. It towers to a peak, from above which God looks benignly down upon the praying figure of John. Weight uses all the gradations of the medium, ranging from jet to the white ground of the paper. Rays of light in straight beams emanate from the image of God and run down the side of the mountain, to fall upon the praying hands of the Baptist. Simple in symbolism and dignified in design, it is a sufficient adjunct to the text.

Water pours from a high rock, refreshing those who sit underneath. It exemplifies the mercies of the Exodus, which the Israelites are exhorted to remember. A woman hastens. She points to the water and, turning her head to others unseen behind her, encourages them to hurry. Those at the waterfall indicate, by their several attitudes and expressions, relief, gratitude, anxiety. One, lolling back against the rock, is evidently complacent. A design of varied interest: achieved in a few exiguous lines of the pen.

The Promise of Restoration is fulfilled by one who, beneath a bridge, is receiving baptism from John. A few spectators are perched on the bridge, idly dangling their feet over the parapet. They look on as others, anxious for baptism, pick their way down to the water. One has stopped half-way down and, embarrassed by the witnesses, hesitates to remove his clothes – a charming touch, catching the optimism of the text:

> Ho, everyone that thirsteth, come ye to the waters!
>
> (Chapter 55)

Contemporary images stress the timeless relevance of the pronouncement on the relief of the poor. An old couple stand in a torrential downpour. The old woman holds a huge metal bowl in which she catches the rain. The old man raises his face into the rain, and prays. His face is dignified and trustful, hers more concerned with the practical need to catch as much water as possible.

> When the poor and needy seek water and there is none, and their tongue faileth for
> thirst, I the Lord will hear them.
>
> (Chapter 41)

*The Crucifixion* illustrates 'He bore the sins of many', and is based on the large painting of 1959. Calvary, more hand-like than ever, has now acquired a massive forefinger and thumb between which it holds up a single cross. As in 1959 the view is from behind, and the arms only are visible on the crossbeam (Chapter 53).

Weight courageously depicts the naked image of God. The viewpoint is once again from behind the figure. The body is chunky and the arms elongated, but the buttocks are tiny, and the overall impression is not convincing. He stands on some parapet which, I take it, overlooks the Mundane Universe, and He reaches up his left arm into the centre of the sun. Something may be owing here to Blake's well-known figure of Urizen, the frontispiece to *Europe, A Prophecy*. Weight's design carries nothing of the suggestive power of Blake's, or of the text.

> I am the Lord, and there is nothing else. I form the light and create darkness.
> (Chapter 45)

Concentric circles are superimposed upon the subjects of two pictures to convey the notion of timelessness, of the projecting forward of the prophecy into the present. In the first, animals – some more attentive to the Centre than others – illustrate 'The beast of the field shall honour me' (Chapter 43). In their midst, with eyes raised towards the Centre, a man kneels in prayer. He is in modern dress, but could represent those who, through the centuries, have taken up the mantle of St Francis. Two hard-headed men of the world are walking away with their backs turned to the Centre – the 'still point', 'the heart of light'.[10]

In the second picture (opposite), modern man is again the hero. He mounts the steps of an imposing staircase, with his little daughter on his shoulder, his energetic ascent drawn with an appropriately sturdy line. The circles through which we look at the design could reflect the circularities of Purgatory,[11] the timeless character of spiritual aspiration. The relevant text is

> They shall bring thy sons in their arms, and thy daughters shall be carried upon their
> shoulders. (Chapter 49)

The child, thus carried, clings to the man's hair, apprehensive, so purposefully does he stride upward. It is a charming touch, a foil to the powerfully symbolic action expressed in such vigorous physical terms.

> And all thy children shall be taught of the Lord. (Chapter 54)

This text suggested a study of innocence, and the teaching here is that of the Ancient Mariner – that loving all creatures is the best form of prayer.

A little family has gathered round a pond. The young mother, or elder sister, stoops and feeds the ducks, watched by the youthful father and three small boys. Two of these, having bathed in the pond, are in the nudity of Innocence. One, however, stands apart, outside the attention father is lavishing upon his brothers, and he is shivering – more from jealous anger than from cold. No doubt the situation will soon be happily resolved. It is a charmingly truthful study of a family knowing as much happiness as humankind can bear.

We might suspect there were times when the grandeur of thought was too lofty to follow. Carel Weight sought no easy way out via abstraction. He faced the difficulties head-on, and, in the main, produced adequate and convincing variations on the text. His qualifying words on the commission were as follows:

> Once they were finished, I was rather glad I'd taken them on. But some of the things I
> wouldn't normally have wanted to do.

# 7

## THROUGH THE SIXTIES II
### Fantasy
### Observations of the Psyche
### Minor Landscapes

The things he would normally want to do were outside the demands of literature. These lay within — with that visionary reflection of reality we know as the world of Carel Weight.

The sixties were marked by the dismantling of old principles and arrangements. Impressionable youth rebelled against traditional values, obsessed with 'doing one's thing'.[1]

Of course, artists of any worth must also 'do their own thing' — never too easy in the past, when patronage had too strong a say. Carel Weight — one of those elect ones to whom 'doing his thing' was the very life-blood — could only sympathise with the new bearings and aspirations of the young.

That sympathy surfaces easily enough today, despite his eighty-five years. I called once at his studio, to be admitted by a young lady whose tutorial with Weight had just ended. He introduced her as an artist of great promise.

Evidently a social function was imminent, which both were to attend and which demanded formality of dress. She promised to be carefully turned out for the occasion, and that he'd be proud to be with her, so very different and impressive would be her appearance.

'Does that mean,' said Carel, 'that you'll be wearing another pair of dungarees with differently arranged frayings and tears?'

She kissed him an affectionate goodbye with a promise: 'You'll see!' She was a young lady of much charm, and I doubt if she failed her promise.

**Fury (1961)**
*Oil on canvas, 36 × 48in (91.4 × 122cm),*
*Herbert Art Gallery, Coventry.*

That Vasari-like story affords a glimpse into that quick sympathy with the young which students of those wayward years so warmly acknowledge.

By the late sixties things had become intolerable at the Royal College of Art. Practices developed which only the daftest anarchist could approve – such as discarding the brush in favour of the bicycle, and riding the thing over wet canvases. Weight told Michael Rooney:

> I had to stop it, there was a lot of pitch on the floor and I felt at any moment the whole of the RCA would go up in flames. I felt at the end of that terrible year [1968] I was going to resign because I had no sympathy with those sorts of things. I used to think that perhaps they'd get somewhere – it was just a necessary stage to go through, and so I tried to be as bold as I could about it. . . It seemed to be going back to a sort of chaos.

There was much pleading from friends and authorities to prevent his taking early retirement. The wonder was that all this did not interfere with his output of original work. But the academic life and the life of the artist belonged to separate compartments.

'I was very lucky,' he told me. 'I could turn my mind from some academic problem, and put it to one side and get on with my painting. A lot of people don't seem to be able to do that, but I've always been able to, and that's been a great help.'

The decade which began with *The Masterstroke of Dr Tarbusch* (1960, page 120) ended with the *Head of Medusa* (page 79) and *Despair* (page 81), both of 1969. The same malaise accounts for *The Friends* (1968, page 85) and the studies of neurotic subjects.

Artistically, it was all grist to his mill. The ferment of the period threw up the things he would 'normally want to paint'. For life was no longer the charted adventure of many, but its courses were eccentric, illusory, nerve-racked. It found its reflection in the world of Carel Weight.

In *The Masterstroke of Dr Tarbusch* (1960) the conjuror produces lots of odd characters from his hat, and these adumbrate the oddities which were to follow. The oddities would belong as much to reality as to phantasmagoria. In fact, they emerged more and more from reality as the decade advanced. For instance, there's something very strange in the straightforward architectural record of *Natural History* (1963). Two queer customers are the protagonists of *Man and Skeleton* (1966, page 79), and *Thoughts of the Girls* (1967, page 82) integrates wildly disparate images of obsessive dreams. *The Friends* is a picture of the intense and destructive force of friendship in the tragic world of abnormal psychology.

Dr Tarbusch conjures up an army of weird shapes, emblematic of the irrational world. Indeed, some may represent punitive agents we might encounter elsewhere!

Concerning his own world, Weight has spoken of the importance of the relationship between background and character which point is clearly demonstrated in *Fury* (1961, opposite), where the setting is every bit as involved in the action as the *dramatis personae* themselves.

From the vanishing-point, somewhere above the roof of the greenhouse, a drive runs in a widening curve towards us. It is flanked by a spiked fence and a high wall. These are powerful lines, flared to spread across the whole width of the immediate foreground. They insist that we attend to the action – a boy being assaulted, another running in panic from the scene, a workman cringing against the wall and a policeman pedalling urgently to the incident. A loosely circular grouping confines these activities, crucially balanced, within the sweeping curves, the structural basis of the composition. The policeman strains at his handlebars – just a faint scratch of white paint and yet a functional line at the inverted apex of more prominent areas of light. These areas – the white trimmings on the posterns, the sills, eaves and windowframes of the mansion, the grey shine on the greenhouse – define a troubled, thundery atmosphere. Overhead, the clouds are agitated and reach out wavering arms. More sinister still, the trees extend their branches as if to applaud the ferocity of the attack.

Not only is the setting alive in this way, but the main features, sinister and combative, are functionally symbolic, and counterpoint the theme of the composition. The red barrier of the wall, for instance, and spears of the fence palisading a corner of the park: tall trees in the grounds of the mansion standing darkly aloof as audience, others closely assisting the drama with sheltering, sinister branches. All are assigned their stations by a stage manager who knows his job.

'*Fury* is very much a study in menace,' Weight said, 'with the frightening tentacles of branches intruding to enlarge the idea of violence.'

**First Landing on Earth (1964)**
*Oil on canvas, 36 × 27in (91.4 × 68.5cm), private collection.*

**Hamlet (1965)**
*Oil on board, 26 × 20in (66 × 50.1cm),*
*Robin Bynoe collection.*

It was all he said, but how rich the experience to have been taken through the work, stage by stage!

We know he works quickly, and once the first rushed strokes were sketched we may imagine with what excitement the full painting was realised.

Very recently (1991) he led me to the latest things he was doing. In one, a hedgerow was a rush of green paint and I felt compelled to question the speed of the brush. 'It looks as if your brush was in a tremendous hurry. Is that the case – does it "hurry"?'

The laconic answer: 'I only wish it did!'

Linearity gives force and direction to the action of *The Death of Lucretia* (1963). It is staged at the end of the parallel runs of flowered border, trellised wall and garden path. Other features are quiescent. Trees soften the harsh outlines of the houses, which seem to recoil from the scene they overlook. The houses in Carel Weight are personages, like Munch's, and here we might imagine they are sustaining a choric role, providing their mute, elegiac comment.

Only a strip of Lucretia's house is visible. Utterly commonplace and austere, it is, for all that, the pivot of Roman history. The pathway pulls Lucretia to the end of the garden, which offers the spectator the best possible view of her heroic example – preferring death to living in unchastity.

If we contrast this picture with *Fury* – where action and setting are closely harmonised – we may see how discreetly Carel Weight treated this episode of classical history.

Lucretia takes her life in Carel Weight's garden, so familiar yet his 'unending source of inspiration'. Familiarity breeds the unusual and gives authenticity and cogency to the extreme acts we witness.

The opening chapters of Wells' *War of the Worlds* (1898) gave Weight the idea for his *First Landing on Earth* (1964, page 77). He sets his scene in the backyard of his home in Battersea, and by so doing he was well and truly in the territory of the book. It is on Putney Hill – right in the heart of Carel Weight's London – that we are given the apocalyptic vision of the earth under the Martians. The homely terrain of both Wells and Carel Weight convinces us of the authenticity of what we are told and what we are shown.

A flight of stone steps ascends from ground level to a stone landing – there is a punning sense in the title reminiscent of Cruikshank[2] – giving access to the house. On the first step a man is stumbling in panic flight. Across the landing his wife scuttles for the door and safety. A neighbour leans out from her upstairs window and stares skyward. In the basement area another woman peers up, fascinated and transfixed.

Dynamic lines – the zigzagging, white-painted edge of the staircase and balcony – lend impetus to the rush for safety. The two staring women – one from her upstairs window, the other from the area – are points of physical stasis, not mental, between which the action drives furiously on landing and staircase. Stasis and action, in such positive counterbalance, give tremendous stress to the ideas of panic flight and petrified terror.

Carel Weight's work seldom reflects contemporary events – *The Battersea Park Tragedy* (1974, page 92) is an exception – but now, in the middle and later sixties, the moral distemper spreads to such canvases as *Thoughts of the Girls* (1967), *The Friends* (1968) and *Despair* (1969). This Descent to Avernus, marked by acts of violence, psychic disorders, neuroses and self-deception, leads to the culminating horrors of *Despair* and the *Head of Medusa* (1969).

The distemper could have something to do with his choice of *Hamlet* for a series of Shakespeare paintings. In 1964 an *Illustrated Shakespeare* was commissioned, each play to be illustrated by a distinguished artist. Weight was the first to be approached, and was given first choice to induce him to accept. His immediate choice was *Hamlet*. He was also asked to advise on how best to allocate responsibility.

Sadly, the project failed through lack of funds – a great disappointment, as he had enjoyed the challenge and finished eighteen pictures by the time it fell through. However, all but one sold, and this – a huge canvas of 6ft 9in (205.7cm) square – he presented to the Harris Museum, Preston.

Another version of *Hamlet* (1965, above) has features in common with the later *Head of Medusa* (1969, opposite). The gravedigger in *Hamlet* and the labourer in the *Medusa*, both stripped to the waist, have unearthed the grisly objects which they thrust up into prominent view. In the first, the clashing areas of light and shade, the craggy banks of rock obtusely angled to the sheer lines of cliff edge presage the violent scene – the struggle in the grave – which is soon to follow. Hamlet, standing removed, looks at the object the gravedigger holds aloft. It is a moment of calm, a prelude of silence before he delivers his 'exequy' on Yorick.

*The Head of Medusa* has about it a marvellously petrified look. All, except the ploughman still intent on driving a straight furrow, are now motionless stone. Ignorant of this, he ploughs on, little suspecting the fate which awaits the turning of his plough.

Other *Hamlet* designs followed. They were of great dramatic power, the result of his sharply sensitive response to the poetry of the play and intuitive understanding of the staging integral to the highly charged relations in the situations he chose. Such deep soundings generated a sequence of impressive designs.

According to A.E. Housman, the restless condition of man, 'the blight man was born for', was due to the bones insistently reminding him of the mortality of the flesh:

> *Wanderers eastward, wanderers west,*
> *Know you why you cannot rest?*
> *'Tis that every mother's son*
> *Travails with a skeleton.*[3]

Weight would turn to Housman twelve years later for an idea, but nothing as solemn as the above stanza was the origin of *Man and Skeleton* (1966, below).

A shambling, untidy man – a casually self-employed model – presented himself at the studio, seeking work.

> He walked in, and stood just as you see him – exactly in the right place. If I'd posed him all morning I couldn't have got it so absolutely right. He was a good model, but was so neglectful of personal care that in summer his feet were aromatic and he could only be employed on a seasonal basis. In summer I would refrain from using him. . . This was the first of many paintings I did of him. As for the skeleton – it was always being maltreated by students, so I kept it in my room. It's a play between the man and the skeleton. It stands close to him, and there are certain points of departure between them.

**The Head of Medusa (1969) (detail)**
*Oil on panel, 120 × 48in (304.8 × 121.9cm),*
*Robin Bynoe collection.*

**Man and Skeleton (1966)**
*Oil on canvas, 48 × 72in (121.9 × 182.8cm),*
*Frank Manzi collection.*

The door stands open, as the ultimate portal through which the old man will pass in abdication to his interior *doppelgänger* – 'The steadfast and enduring bone.' Yet it's an anatomical specimen, and no more than that. Its knock-knees and feet could shuffle and slip on the stand and the structure sag and collapse. Something comic could be suggested in its good-humoured grin – as near as it gets to the grisly enjoyment of its compeers in Holbein, Bosch and Bruegel.

But no – it's not a comfortable picture. The *memento mori* stands between two of Weight's disturbing pictures. One is a fraught subject of some psychological upheaval under a sky a-rush with wind. The other is of a huge ear – a sinister motif from *The Land of Ears* (*c*.1961), a wartime fantasy on the obsession with secrecy and silence in a world where the common virtues are inverted.

*Despair* (1969, opposite) takes us into the Nordic gloom of abnormal psychology. It is to follow Munch's lead of seventy years earlier, but Weight's exposition is no less authoritative. The room is dingy, high-ceilinged and empty, except for the chair occupied by the poor, desolated fellow. It is very like one of those cell-like wards for the temporary isolation of the deeply disturbed. A grim-looking female, possibly his mother, is leaving the room. Her mouth is open, and she could be weeping.

The dramatist in Carel Weight handles his entrances and exits with supreme confidence. Here, again, the opening door stresses the ephemeral nature of experience – an interpretation deriving from Bede's famous parable,[4] comparing the present life of man to the swift passage of a sparrow through a lighted hall

> coming in by one door and going out by the other. For the time for which he is within, the bird is sheltered from the storm, but after this short while of calm he flies out again into the cold and is heard no more.

An unpretty kettle of fish – nothing venerable attaching – crowds the door in *Thoughts of the Girls* (1967, page 82). 'These two,' said Weight, 'had entirely different obsessions which I wanted to show in the same picture.'

The device he used reminded me of those vignettes, so beautifully executed by 'Phiz' as frontispieces for Dickens.

A young lady, sensuously attractive, enters a room. She opens the door on another plain interior. In the right-hand corner, huddled in her chair, sits the second girl, looking profoundly dejected. Both are wearing the mini-skirt of the period, which raises the sensual temperature of the picture.

The girl at the door is backed by a host of ugly visitants, among them a skeleton. In fact, we have the elements of the *Vanitas* – quite in the manner of Bosch. These, the *phantasiae personae*, appear in a miasmal whirl of ectoplasm. Spikily brushed lines streak from them into the room, mingling with the fumes eddying about the oriental images which embody the thoughts of the seated girl.

Downcast in her chair, she dreams of a luxurious life as illusory as the East. A splendidly robed emir stands before a glorious mosque with towering minarets. But his head is offset by the skeleton skull which obtrudes from round the frame of the door. Below that, a leering profile emerges from near the potentate's shoulder, mouth gaping in demoniacal laughter. Next, a masked face is attentive to the sensual lure of the girl at the door. It could betoken folly, even insanity, but more likely, lust. A blanched face, whites of eyes gleaming, looks directly at us to imply that we are not free from such *ignes fatui* ourselves. Two other *grilli* portray envy and wrath.

The seated girl closes her eyes and, with hands tightly clasped and pressed between her knees, bends forward under the incubi of her wishes. These, like a mirage, are fading as the door opens to reveal the chimeras which haunt her friend. In that mass there is a Dalí-like subtle confusion of appearances, tricking our vision. A dimple on an ugly chin serves also as the eye of a foxy, hyaena-like creature with long, tubular muzzle – a very Bosch-like image.

'It's a kind of surrealist idea,' said Carel Weight. 'Both were my students. One dreamt of getting out to the East, where she had a boyfriend. The other was obsessed with ideas of black magic. I just called it *Thoughts of the Girls*.'

It was all he said. But it is not a composition where the issues are sharply contrasted, as between darkness and light. The thoughts of the girls derive from a common source of unrest – dissatisfaction with the way things are, and magic is invoked as the means of escape. Whatever the nature of the magic – black or glaring white – it is potent to confuse and mislead. Consequently, the images are merging, shifting towards a synthesis in

**Despair (1969)**
*Oil on panel, 120 × 48in (304.8 × 121.9cm),*
*Bernard Jacobson Gallery.*

the swirling ectoplasm. For the moment, however, resolution is suspended – a condition deliberately unsatisfactory for the spectator.

What an impact these large figures have upon him! He is keyed-up with questions, the first of which must address the nature of the resolution, once the images fuse and vanish and work-a-day senses prevail, and communication between the girls is restored.

In *The Silence* (1965, above) the partitions of the weatherboard fence range in cell-like units three members of a family. Each is locked into his or her separate worlds. A distant roof displays a television aerial – too often the enemy of social intercourse. A church spire enjoins silence for the utterance of the dogmatic, unchallenged pronunciation.

> I have always felt that no matter how close you are to your friends or lovers, you are, in fact, a solitary person. Perhaps I enjoy being on my own – but no. No, I'm not commenting on that, at all.
>
> It's a separateness – here are three individuals, all quite different, all perfectly still.
>
> It's always seemed eerie to me – the two minutes' imposed silence on Remembrance Day. And especially so if it's broken by a dog in the distance somewhere, bewildered by it all. . . The three in this little family are observing the silence, each one locked away in a world of his or her own.

**The Silence (1965)**
*Oil on panel, 36 × 48in (91.4 × 121.9cm),*
*Artist's Diploma Picture for the Royal*
*Academy / Royal Academy of Arts Library.*

**(Opposite)**
**Thoughts of the Girls (1967)**
*Oil on canvas, 66 × 53in (167.6 × 134.6cm),*
*Saatchi Collection, London.*

**Thoughts of Girlhood (1968)**
*Oil on canvas, 36 × 48in (91.4 × 121.9cm),*
*Collection of Lady Delacourt-Smith / Royal*
*Academy of Arts Library.*

Weight's principal model for *Thoughts of the Girls* posed also for his two *Tense Girl* studies. All three pictures belong to 1967. *Thoughts of Girlhood* (1968, above) carries the theme forward to the poignant later days of a woman's life. There we see the tragic isolation of the elderly relieved in the shape of the woman's reflections – a voluptuous version of her younger self who, by right of her charms, could claim the general attention. It is a sad progression to the *Despair* of 1969 via these tensed-up girls and lonely old woman, and it takes us into the taut, tragic situation of *The Friends* (1968, opposite).

I phoned the painter to consult him on the picture. I was about to lecture on modern painters and was to include some mention of *The Friends*. He was happy enough with what I was thinking – that the uncurtained windows suggested a removal, that the friends were on the point of parting, that the situation was tragic. Of course, the child's question was wholly expected: who were these 'friends'? Weight suggested that if I supposed the relationship were intense, it would not be far wrong – 'As between lesbians.'

The room is austere. On the cabinet between the windows are two heavy black candlesticks, their tall candles unlighted. In the cabinet some companion volumes are bleak with a dead, unopened look. The uncurtained windows suggest (ironically) spring, or preparations for moving. Indeed, they may have just moved in. A light has been switched on and then, it seems, a situation arose. The light falls on a figurine on its shelf, and this could have been the first object unpacked and put in its place as a token of determined optimism in an uncertain relationship. Or it might indicate that the friendship has been stormy and combative. The woman nearer the observer, with face in profile, seems stricken, the result of her partner's resolve, or changed attitude. The other supports her head on her shoulder, and looks out across the room, her expression determined yet compassionate.

We should accept the work as a study of a relationship, and discard any thought of narrative. 'They were two poorish women,' he told me many years later when we resumed discussion. It was at a time when social taint attached to their condition. 'When, in fact, they were complete outcasts. I wanted, above all, to convey their loneliness.' It is in no way a double portrait. The heads are purely visionary, and the concern was to indicate a situation, and nothing more.

We note that in *Fallen Woman* (1967, page 86) the intruding greenery droops and is scanty, and that the Old Lady in *Thoughts of Girlhood*, painted the next year, 1968, is fairly embowered with greenery in full leaf, and

white roses spring up and incline above her. She sits bemused as the spectre of her former self steals away in a long, low-cut dress which gives formidable prominence to the deep bosom.

But the *Fallen Woman* has no such ghosts, either for regret or entertainment. She ponders her history, which needs no outer projection, for sad experience is written deeply in the worn eyes under their heavy lids. There is a chastened look, a resignation to her fate, as if that were due more to external constraints than to her own fault. But there has been struggle, so that like Anatole France's fallen woman

> she began, under sadness and regret, to acquire a look of spiritual beauty.[5]

Posed in the open door of a garden outhouse, she is offset and 'exposed' by the steel legs of the chair and some framework which intrudes from the right. The bare lattice on her left appears to be of the same cold metal. The yellowish brickwork – dark inside the recess behind her – is unpleasing, even depressing.

Despite her general air of defeat, there is the look of being ready to spring to her own defence, and determination and guile can be traced in the strong, coarse-lipped mouth and hard, firm chin.

Even so, her dress resembles a nun's habit, opened a little, but enough to show the long scarlet streak of the dress beneath; a bold enough display to distract attention from her guilt.

Tragically, her history is one of temptation and guilt.

**The Friends (1968)**
*Oil on panel, 60 × 81in (152.4 × 205.7cm),*
*Tate Gallery, London.*

**Fallen Woman (1967)**
*Oil on panel, 40 × 23in (101.6 × 58.4cm),*
*John Brandler collection / RA Library.*

**Portrait of Jane I (c.1961)**
*Oil on canvas, 40 × 30in (101.6 × 76.2cm),*
*Royal Pavilion Art Gallery and Museums,*
*Brighton.*

She was a model, very inexperienced. In fact, I may well have given her her first sitting . . . I was interested in her voice, which was soft and educated. I posed her at the end of my garden. Eventually, I heard her story. She'd held some position of responsibility in a home for women who'd fallen on bad times. Some mismanagement of affairs and funds led to her dismissal. She decided she'd be a model. In a way she was 'superior' – not liking to be lumped in with all 'the other girls'. I don't suppose she was very nice, but her face really did look as if she'd had a great deal of suffering. I suppose she felt disgraced. I don't quite know what she felt. I found her very interesting to paint.

Artefacts which help to establish mood and character are chosen with the discretion and fine judgment of a poet. For instance, the *Hungarian Woman* (1962) is backed firmly by the solid mantelpiece, with a figurine flanked by elaborate candlesticks; her sensitive, practical face has its sturdy, altar-like support.

In *Portrait of Jane I* (c.1961, below left) the long arms, the slim graceful figure, are echoed in the lines of a chair and china cabinet. She sits a little forward of these, so that their place in the composition is given a secondary importance, and Jane herself sticks vividly off from these, ardent, bright and charming. With wrists and hands in a strained tension between her knees, she sits under the artist's scrutiny in the neurosis of her submission.

Perhaps I have been too concerned to show how Weight's subjects reflected the wayward trends of the decade. If now the strain is altered to one which is lighter, more restful and reflective, it should lead more naturally to his gesture of tender defiance to the turpitude of the decade in *Two Figures and a Statue* (1969, right).

Visits to friends in West Sussex and the north of Suffolk gave him the quiet he needed through these turbulent years, and provided him with subjects for numerous landscapes. Most of these are in very small format. Several were painted in the neighbourhood of Sutton (West Sussex).

One which remains *Untitled* (right) belongs to 1962, and boldly contrasts a ponderous foreground of deep wintry tints with the pale, slightly lifting fields reaching away to the horizon. We overlook a sunken road under an immensely high embankment, beyond which we glimpse the fields with the requisite rural accessories – cattle, either at rest or grazing, a thatched cottage with paddock and piled hop-poles. Trees offer sporadic greenery in the face of winter's dearth. The austerity of the season is implied by the heavy clothing worn by the couple in the narrow sunken road. Their faces are set, unrelaxed, and they walk along, separated by almost the entire width of the road.

The subject was repeated the next year in *Two Figures in a Landscape* (1963). Again, emphasis is on the sunken road above which we look across a much reduced stretch of autumnal landscape. And, once again, two heavily clad figures, a man and woman, seem to be walking together as if under constraint of custom.

Landscapes, also miniature in scale, resulted from visits to that northern part of Suffolk where the quiet reliefs induce subtleties of light and shade, the landscape of atmosphere. But these visits were brief, and Weight was content with the swiftly caught impression rather than with any exploration into the nuances which preoccupied the East Anglian School. Such an impression – it cannot be classed as landscape – is the charming *The Mill Stream* (1963). A girl and an old man stroll on the towpath – she, lightly dressed; he, with care, as befits old age. The buildings catch the sun; the mill house roof, mirror-like, shines grey under a thinly clouded sky.

*The Poet's Muse* (c.1964) belongs to both landscape and genre. The characters, in a very special relationship, are persons of a drama, not simply figures in a landscape. The picture reflects a happy mood induced by a period of repose in rural England.

In the background, a Cornish tin mine, chimney stack probing the sky. The Poet, cloth-capped and Sunday-suited, stands, centre of the picture, where two footpaths meet – between the girl of his poems and his Muse.

The effulgent moment – if indeed, there was one – must have lapsed suddenly, for the Muse, winged and classically draped, floats away via the other path on the right. She lifts a hand to her face, sad that she has failed in her office, which was, first, to inspire and, second, to sustain the rhapsodic exercise. Maybe she pleads with her father, the President of Olympus, for a recall to Parnassus. I suggest she is Erato, Muse of erotic poetry, sent by Zeus in his usual jocular vein, to assist the Poet. The circumstances were propitious – two converging souls, their pathways meeting, under the upreared chimney.

Meanwhile, the subject of the Poet's intended rhapsody – a tubby little soul who could derive from

Bruegel's *Peasant's Wedding* – looks towards the Poet, comically expectant.

The decade ends on a note of reconciliation, for besides *Despair* (page 81) we must reckon with *Two Figures and a Statue*.

The little statue opposes its youth to the infirmity of ageing flesh. An old man, his arm laid tenderly across his wife's shoulders, leads her from the statue, a memorial to their daughter who died young. But the statue stands, thigh-deep in flowers, and with double-edged irony points the power of ephemeral, human love in opposition to the triumph of time.

**Two Figures and a Statue (1969)**
*Oil on panel, 36 × 36in (91.4 × 91.4cm),*
*private collection.*

**Untitled (1962)**
*Oil on board, 20 × 24in (50.8 × 60.9cm),*
*Bernard Jacobson Gallery.*

# 8

## A PORTFOLIO OF THE SEVENTIES
### The Human Predicament
### Elegiac and Religious Pieces
### Hauntings and the Mystical – Portraiture

---

He is attentive to the years, resigned to things as they are, expectant of what may still be accomplished. Such may be our impressions of Weight's *Portrait of the Artist in a Cold Studio* (1974, below). The bland expression verges on a smile, whose full indulgence the cold inhibits.

Since 1972, on retiring from the Royal College of Art, Carel Weight's life had settled to happy, creative courses. Retirement came with a relief he could only compare with the way he felt on leaving the army, twenty-two years since. But the relief was tempered by the tragedy in Battersea Park – the accident to the Big Dipper, with the deaths of five children and injuries to many more. He was moved profoundly, to the compassion of *The Battersea Park Tragedy* (1974, page 92). It is his finest elegy.

As he looked back over the last decade of teaching, it must have seemed that a new and darker currency had been given those besetting miseries of insularity and isolation. The infamous 'age gap' opened and widened. The divisions figured in *The Silence* (1965, page 83) were now embodied in the dead-alive characters of *The World We Live In* (1970–3, opposite). Theirs is an ironic alfresco setting, a *'zone de tristesse'*[1] very different from the ordered garden of their middle-class counterparts of *The Silence*. They have strayed into an area filled with the debris of years of neglect, and here they are brought to a halt and paraded for our inspection. Two men in the foreground – one middle aged, the other a youth – present the horror of empty lives, hopes thwarted, or drugged into confused despair. A third figure, a woman, half turns her back on them, indifferent,

**Portrait of the Artist in a Cold Studio (1974)**
*Oil on canvas, 14½ × 28½in (36.8 × 72.3cm), Sir Brinsley Ford collection.*

and with her own purposeless ways to pursue. The youth in the centre of the group hangs his head and closes his eyes against the light. Next to him, the older man stands propped on stiff, scarecrow-like legs, the epitome of self-neglect. An old boater, angled jauntily off the brow, is a sad relic of smarter days. He looks at us, but avoids our eye with the dulled, lugubrious expression of a dead soul. 'Regard these closely,' the painter might advise, 'the horror of the drifting, unawakened life.'

Instruction so direct is by no means the first intention – which is to appeal to the viewer's compassion, nothing more. But we may regard the picture as an object lesson and derive from it as much instruction as we choose. It is a sorry parade, like those of Lowry's *Cripples* or *Funeral Party* and, like them, not intended to be didactic.

1971 produced *A Memory of Childhood*, a twilit, melancholy scene recalling a walk with his father. 1972 began with a sequence of fraught subjects – *Haunted House*, *Trying on Masks* and *Votive Picture* following each other in swift succession. A gloomy, macabre collection. The disaster in Battersea Park occurred the same year. It was high time Weight found relief in a subject which would give free rein to his quirky humour. He chose *The Assumption of the Virgin* (1972, page 90) and his own terraced street as the setting for the frenzied reaction to the miracle.

A tunnelled passage – a 'shared access' in estate agents' parlance – to the rear of a terrace block concentrates our attention upon the reaction of two men who peer skyward, transfixed by the miracle. A youth with wildly tousled hair rushes out towards us, escaping from the scene. Opposite, across the street, someone leans out of the bedroom window and looks up astounded.

Only the cord of the Virgin's dressing-gown floats down, very likely to be caught by one of the men, whose hands are raised in readiness.

The passageway enforces our own 'shared access' to the miracle and ourselves to co-operate with the onlookers in giving to the humble cord something of its spiritual charge. Hemmed in by the narrowness of the passage, the chief witnesses can only stand stock-still, gaping. Their turmoil of soul is conveyed by the youth bursting out in panic from the scene.

A poet of the ordinary, Weight will admit nothing more to his suburban *Assumption* than the Virgin's cord, the only relic of the 'heavenly garments which the Father had sent to shroud Mary in'.[2]

His instinct for humour nudges him strongly here – to spiritualise the cord of a dressing-gown, to galvanise two men awaiting its descent like cricketers expecting a difficult catch in the nightmare straits of a 'shared access'.

There is nothing sententious in these religious subjects.

*The Rest on the Flight into Egypt* and *The Last Judgement* came the next year, 1973 – small panels, well-suited to his intimate versions of subjects familiar to us on the grander scales of the Old Masters.

*The Last Judgement* (page 91) is reduced to centre upon three representatives who, having passed through Judgement into the Ranks of the Blessed, dance exuberantly in expectation of Paradise. A few others queue up in the distance for their ordeal in the striped marquee. This picture is, in fact, the fully developed version of the sketch painted twelve years previously, and briefly mentioned in Chapter 6.

In a striking example of Weight's best Mannerist style, his heroine – a well-proportioned lady in the centre – pulls at a dragging hand which would haul her out of the picture. The hand enters from outside the right frame, and grips her wrist tightly. We do not see its owner. In the delighted dance her beads fling out, her body twists. She plants her left and leading foot flat on the ground – an anchorage too weak against the wonderful power we suspect. For she'd stay in the centre if she could, for as long as it takes to show off her newly won bliss. 'We shall be changed in the twinkling of an eye', a moment so sudden that those who have undergone the change doubt that it has indeed overtaken them. So she holds back – earthly shortcomings persisting – to show off to whom it may concern how she feels to have come through the Last Judgement with credit.

Dragged up on to the ball of her right foot, she will soon topple out of the picture altogether, an involuntary movement which wrenches on the hesitant male whose hand she is holding. He cannot believe his luck. Linked in a ring, as in the children's game, they dance round in an endless dance of delight, but with joyless, immobile faces stunned by the tremendous nature of the verdict. There could be points of contact with the circulating Cavalcade of the Sensuous in Bosch's *Garden*. The well-endowed heroine generates energy, while her partner, submissive to her pressures, is the epitome of one who, in earthly life, never expected much. A touching and powerful moment. In the background a queue moves resignedly to Judgement, in contrast with the

**The World We Live In** (1970–73)
*Oil on panel, 48 × 37in (121.9 × 93.9cm),*
*Arts Council Collection, The South Bank*
*Centre, London / John Webb FRPS.*

**The Assumption of the Virgin (1972)**
*Oil on panel, 43 × 32½in (109.2 × 82.5cm),*
*Bradford Art Gallery.*

abandoned, contorted movement in front. As complement to the whole, the bunting flaps and dances overhead in counterpoint to the turmoil of awakening souls.

*The Rest on the Flight into Egypt* is a delightful 'quietude'. Mary nurses the baby as the evening gathers and Joseph lights his pipe. Even the donkey is absent, so that nothing detracts from the little family in its silent concentration – Mary on the child, Joseph on his lighter. Under its flame – the one point of strong illumination – Joseph's face is thoughtful as the lighter rekindles the symbol of the Nativity.

From the end of May 1972, when the tragic accident took place in Battersea Park,[3] Weight had considered a picture based on the event. The idea for the picture reached him as an immediate vision, and matured slowly under his painstaking craftsmanship. Two years following the event, his large canvas *The Battersea Park Tragedy* (page 92) was shown at the Royal Academy Exhibition of 1974.

To appreciate this deeply compassionate work, we should attempt some understanding of its demands.

There had to be a sombre chromatic range. The prominent green had to be lowered close to the tone of the yew. The bluish-grey of the tennis courts was made a quiet foil to the near-purple of the solitary mourner, whose black armband explains her presence. The sky is swathed with an ochre band, through which a whitish patch appears on the left. To the right it is streaked and touched with the dominant red.

It was a demanding subject – the deaths of five children on the Big Dipper at the Battersea Park Fun Fair. Two essential elements had to be recognised – the fearful nature of the disaster, and the inconsolable grief which followed. Weight faced the problem courageously, presenting the two elements in a statement both emphatic and restrained.

The mourner stands slightly off-centre, with the tennis courts behind. On the enclosing wire, a notice regulates bookings and ironically associates sport and relaxation with death and mourning. The Big Dipper, designed for pleasure, has become the instrument of pain. The straights and curves of its rails are scratched redly against the sky or plunge into a brushwood tangle of wintry stems. Arc lamps stretch up like toadstools on immensely high wiry stalks and follow the aerial course of the disastrous tracks. Immediately above the trees a spread of white sky is washed with ochre, against which the toadstool caps make a buoyant impression.

Over the tennis courts and leaving the picture, or about to vanish into the ochre and faintly opal sky, appears a strongly built youth, winged and with hands crossed over eyes and forehead as if intensely distressed. The apparition hovers directly above the woman. In the workings of her stricken soul appears the image of one dear to her, a son no doubt. He is there, an angel, in all the strength of youth, voiceless and unseen, grieving that communication is possible only in prayer.

The two strike the deepest chord of elegy and crystallise the tragedy in the sharpest and most direct terms.

**The Last Judgement (1973)**
*Oil on board, 52 × 32in (132 × 81.2cm),
Mr and Mrs Alfred Mignano collection.*

*O souvenirs, printemps, aurore!*[4]

*The Shower* follows his revisiting the park the next year, 1975. It overtakes him near the lane between the shrubbery and the high tennis-court wire. The park is significant to Carel Weight, as there he first came to an awareness of the world about him. Rose had taken him there many times in his pram, and afterwards as a toddler. There he had his first experience of the noisy old aeroplane in the early years of the century. And there he glimpsed that solitary mourner standing by the courts where the present shower detains him.

In 1974 – the year of his cold-studio portrait – there appeared two baleful Nordic influences, and though Carel Weight admires them he is innocent of their cynicism. All along we have been aware of his admiration for Munch, nor do we overlook what he said to Bernard Sternfield: that Strindberg and himself shared 'a similar bent', their distinctive 'atmospheres' creating heightened versions of the real world.[5]

*The Haunted House* (1972), with all its lights blazing, might well have Norse foundations, and be tenanted by neurotic girls! We could find the spirit of Munch in *The sunset itself is such that one cannot tell if this is the end of the day or of the world* (1974) and in *The Invocation* (1976), which had its origin in a sudden scream heard shattering the peace of the Sussex countryside in which he was walking.

Munch's famous *Scream* (1893) came from within, and that is the great difference. Uttered by those blood-red tongues of cloud, it echoed throughout all external nature. ('I felt as though the whole of nature was screaming – screaming in my blood.') But the scream in Weight's *Invocation* came from *outside*, and within the range of ordinary experience.

A year later, and a little smudge of Strindberg might sully a corner of the idyllic garden in *The Song of the Bird* (1977). Indeed, Strindberg, writing in 1907 on his play *The Ghost Sonata*, describes to a 'T' the painful situation of the Ghost in *I Cheer a Dead Man's Sweetheart* (1978): 'It is horrible like life, when the veil falls from our eyes and we see things as they are.'[6]

But Weight's treatment of the Housman episode is equivocal. The ghost's appealing expression is either the stuff of tragedy or the very staple of comedy and farce. Its tragi-comical mood is without a trace of the obsessive despair of either Housman or Strindberg. In fact, little in Carel Weight is tinged with the darkness of Munch's myth of *Alpha and Omega*, or with Strindberg's warped view of women – a view, however, which he describes energetically in *Strindberg* (1974).

'It's a very odd picture, I must say,' – his reaction to my showing him a photo of *Strindberg*. 'I saw it the other day and thought, "What an odd picture. Whatever made me paint it?" But I'd got interested in Strindberg's plays, which I thought horrific, but very gripping.'

Strindberg stands aloof, looking at two women, one of whom – an auburn-haired girl – embraces the other from behind. Their eyes close in ecstasy, as the embrace strengthens and pulls their bodies together. An immediate impression is that they are locked in rivalry – in the stiffened hold of strenuous conflict. Such an assumption need not be too wide of the mark – rivalries among lesbian lovers nerving and giving thrust to their impassioned exchanges. Strindberg views their act with saddened distaste.

Something may be owing to *The Last Judgement* (above), whose impact is made by the twisted, convulsive heroine at stage centre. But these two abandon themselves to an entirely different ecstasy.

'I've never been to that part of the world.' Weight was referring to Norway and *The World of Edvard Munch* (1975). 'But it seems the picture does capture the atmosphere of Norway. The characters are neurotic and

**The Battersea Park Tragedy (1974)**
*Oil on canvas, 72 × 98in (182.8 × 251.5cm),*
*Arts Centre, Folkestone.*

overwrought. In choosing my colours my purpose was to achieve an intensity, the bright light clashing with a tensed-up human situation.'

Munch's Nordic lights play across the panel, a painting based on a black-and-white photograph of Munch at his easel painting in his garden at Åsgårdstrand. Weight was right to think it would be a good subject for a picture. His painting is an intense, dramatic version of the photo. Colour and some practical alterations make a difference, of course. But he supplies an *angst*, edginess and distraction, absent from the photo, to convey his concept of the female-dominated *World of Edvard Munch*.

Anxious women are watching the flight of a girl who, with hair streaming behind her, rushes from the scene. A sister is seated posing, uneasy and distracted, for her brother. A second stands in the doorway, lost in dreamy reverie. All contribute to create a world wholly divorced from Munch's world of art. He sits hatted and muffled, encased in the self-sufficiency of genius, separate from yet part of the distracted female world under the chill brilliance of the Scandinavian summer.[7]

Certainly, Carel Weight associates the sex with unease, neurotic insecurity, even violence.

The heroines of *Votive Picture* (1972) and *Mrs Rochester* (1973) are vessels of such wrath that one commits murder, the other her murderous assault (*Jane Eyre*, Chapter 26). But at the moment Mrs Rochester is a passive object of representation. 'I thought of that woman all alone in her room high up in the house,' he said. 'A tragic figure, sitting quite still, as mad people do very often. The colours are very intense – pitch black, for instance, against very light tones. But I used a wide range, rather like a pianist using the whole stretch of the keyboard. It's very consciously constructed in a geometric way, like an abstract picture.'

He drew my attention to the lines of door and window, the eaves beyond and other ruled-off, squarish shapes. These features had occupied him exclusively. Nothing of the vampire-nature of the subject had occurred to him, nothing of the Gothic from the Brontë text. *Mrs Rochester* embodied Everyman's essential loneliness – nothing more.

That is the essence which, for me, pervades *The Dress* (1977, page 94). Weight was happy to assent tacitly to that view, but, again, insisted on the importance of composition.

Draped from its line, almost impinging on the arc of the large circular flowerbed, the dress occupies a significant position against the sky and balances the woman in the foreground. A scattering of white blooms

**I Cheer a Dead Man's Sweetheart (1978)**
*Oil on canvas, 36 × 48in (91.4 × 121.9cm),*
*Bernard Jacobson Gallery / Sotheby's,*
*London.*

from some flowering plant curves in to where she stands, a drab, cloth-capped figure tilting the mouth of her bucket towards us. She looks overworked and listless, with her clumsy feet planted firmly in the square shuttering of a disused vegetable frame – one of three such boxes slotted into a parallel run of bricks. These parallels – light ochre and red – with the raised strip of lawn on the right, radiate towards the circular bed like the spokes of a wheel. Diametrically opposite, the short red column of the dress functions as a 'dwell', a point against the sky upon which the eye must pause before returning to the woman via the lines and circularities of the composition. Several other versions of the picture and his *Judith and Holofernes* (*c*.1977) were given the same setting, and show how painstakingly he addressed himself to getting the geometry right. This version pleased him most, and it is not difficult to see why, or why – during our discussion – he should so insist on the importance of the composition.

Red and its derivatives dominate the palette for the autumnal atmosphere, with a greyish white for the flowering plant and the cool sky. Against such tones the elderly woman is funereal in dingy blue, her lethargy made ponderous by the natural features which move restlessly about her. The dress, hanging calmly against the sky, and the woman, stock-still, clumsily set in her frame, are the points of stasis the composition invites us to consider.

I am forced to make an association. That the bowed head, burdened with thought, dwells on a time when, young enough to cut a dash in red, she had made her conquests.

Carel Weight follows the example of Dickens who, out walking, gathered material for his art. A wide expanse of open fields in West Sussex provided him settings for *The sunset is such . . .*, *The Invocation*, *Childhood of a Poet*, and *A Walk with Camille Pissarro* (1976, page 94). The landscape obligingly included a central hut, its gable-end elevation making a useful punctuation in the structure of these pictures. In *A Walk with Camille Pissarro* the hut is a focal point, registering the isolation of the individuals who advance towards us. Intervals of several feet separate one from the other. The slim figure in the centre is Lucien Pissarro in early manhood. Closest to us and a little to the right is Camille Pissarro himself, a bearded savant. On Lucien's left a woman, with head inclined as if constrained by the occasion, shuffles along. The subject is served functionally by this simple disposition. This spacing-out claims for each character in turn a separate attention – a deliberately paced process which lends to each the sense of a leisurely movement forward. The arrangement is symbolic

**A Walk with Camille Pissarro (1976)**
*Oil on panel, 24 × 36in (60.9 × 91.4cm),
private collection.*

as well as dynamic. The woman – unidentified – keeps to the footpath; Lucien strays from the path, as if to diminish the wide gap between himself and his father. The impress of the occasion is ponderous upon the younger figures, too sensible of the divide between youth and age, between genius and talents yet to develop.

Weight was speaking simply, in the most matter of fact way, of practical devices he found effective in the structure of a picture. 'You stand a chance of catching the attention if, in a very realistic picture, you can get away with a piece of fantasy.'

It was the most artless allusion – if allusion it was – to the source of his best, most characteristic poetry: that conflict between an extraordinary event and its commonplace setting. *Barnes Station* (1976, right), where the red brick walls and utilitarian footbridge make an unlikely setting for the spectral child and her vision, is the very essence of this strange poetry. But manifestations of the *'mysterium tremendum et fascinans'*[8] are independent of place, and Barnes Station will accommodate a 'showing' as well as any religious building.

**The Dress (1977)**
*Oil on canvas, 30 × 25in (76.2 × 63.5cm),
private collection.*

In spectral form, a young girl kneels at the vision of the Crucifix. To judge from her long hair and old-fashioned dress, we are witnessing an event experienced by the girl long ago when she was alive. The cross, its figure with raised arms pinned in the bidding to passion, hovers wraith-like above the farther parapet. She is halted in her tracks. Then shock gives way to obeisance – she is bringing her hands together for prayer – to transform the parapet into her *prie-dieu*. The pavement on which the girl kneels twists at the far end to descend to a lower level. A rough compound is formed, well-adapted to contain the small-scale Calvary, a panel of 16 x 18in (40.6 x 45.7cm).

Hands in benediction reach out to *John Wesley in Prayer* (1979), another mystical subject of an even smaller panel (12 x 8in/30.4 x 20.3cm). The hands extend over Wesley from an ill-defined area. Perhaps they're emerging from a humdrum piece of furniture like a wardrobe, or through the wall, conveniently panelled as a point of entry. Yellow walls, red floorings, red streaks under the window, a deep purple sky outside, a black cushioned chair are elements of an excited, Expressionist scheme.

Mervyn Levy reports Carel Weight as follows: 'I filled the room with a feeling of celestial light.' A confident statement, qualified by the next remark: 'My great problem was to prevent the picture seeming too corny.'

The implication could be that coercion was needed to impel the poetic faculty into service, and that it produced something too extravagant for his inclinations, for 'the realistic factor demanded by my own temperament'. Perhaps the 'celestial light' was too Fauvist, or the Hands from the Empyrean too Giottesque for his liking, despite the homeliness of his Empyrean. I took him up on this 'corny' aspect. He replied:

It is a corny subject, of some holy person doing the expected thing. I wanted a miracle to happen, so – he's being blessed by an angel. There's a little annexe to his bedroom – it's quite clearly shown here. He'd pray there every morning and evening. I painted it for the Wesleyans in America.

**Barnes Station (1976)**
*Oil on panel, 16 × 18in (40.6 × 45.7cm),*
*Dr and Mrs Andrew Verney collection.*

Several portraits distinguished the later half of the decade. They were drawn with that characteristic care he spoke of to Norman Rosenthal. There was much linearity, an *estilo frio*, relieved by bold, warm passages of colour. There was even that softer flourish, that smoother application which belonged to the old portrait of *Edna in her Ball-Gown* (1938, page 26). But the linear style serves well his treatment of the tensed-up, uneasy subject.

**Miss Josephine Valentine (1974)**
*Oil on canvas, 36 × 36in (91.4 × 91.4cm),*
*private collection.*

Though cosily seated in the bay window of her lovely home, *Miss Josephine Valentine* (1974, opposite) looks concerned, mindful, maybe, of some unresolved intricacy of her art. She sits, violin and bow in hand – the bow extended to take the eye to the plunged angles of the recess in which she sits. She is flanked on the side opposite the window by the violin case, open to show the bright green baize. Her bow is held in parallel to the upper lateral of the window. The curtain, corded, and pulled back from the window, has affinities in colour and texture with her long concert gown. They billow a little towards her and, with the model, provide a softness against the overall linear severities. Outside, to correspond to Josephine's pose, a stone lion sits solid on his plinth. He is a restriction, a stop to anything irrelevant invading his side of the picture. That, rather than anything symbolic, is his clear function.

> I'd been asked to paint the picture of Helen, Josephine's sister, but some duty intervened to prevent her from keeping the appointment. I turned up with all my equipment, and then Josephine appeared, looking so splendid in her long dress, I just had to paint her instead.

Helen's picture appeared twenty years later in 1993, as a bold Expressionist study of a personality, bright, thinking, and wholly absorbed in her life in art.

We would be ill-advised to make much of the symbolic force of Josephine's lion. As we have seen, it functions as part of the design. The classical laurel-wreathed bust in the *Portrait of an Actor-Poet* (1979) serves both purposes – the symbolic and the functional. The symbolism is obvious; functionally it is a 'stepping-stone' between the brown colour-motifs which run from the sitter's chair to the two framed pictures propped against the wall behind him. It is a tragic portrait of a Man who had Failed. Weight explained:

**Portrait of an Actor-Poet (1979)**
*Oil on canvas, 50 × 50in (127 × 127cm),*
*Metropole Arts Centre, Folkestone.*

> He was a poor fellow who practised neither art successfully. Locally, he was quite well known, and was invited to give a public reading of his poetry in Hammersmith Town Hall. It was very upsetting. I went along to find the place more or less empty. I think he did have something of a gift, but his delivery was so difficult I hardly followed a fraction of what he said. Sadly enough, he died in an Old Persons' Home, which happened to be close to where I lived.

Two paintings are in the background, one standing behind the other. The most prominent is *The World We Live In* (page 89). We see less than a half of the other picture and cannot distinguish the subject. *The World We Live In* is so placed that the sitter's head and shoulders enter its painted foreground, and he becomes the foremost representative of its themes of isolation and decline. His expression shows a deep inward concern, and his hands open as if in resigned acceptance of the World he Lives In.

The drawing is as precise as in a Dürer – the 'wiry bounding' line which William Blake required as a prerequisite for the best work of art. Consequently, the lined face, sharply pointed chin and nose accentuate the concerned, inwardly directed look. So do the poor fellow's accessories: trousers drab and well-worn, cheap tie, ravelled collar, the thin coat of many creases. A red carpet which covers the whole floor gives the subject the prominence he has professionally sought with tragic unsuccess. The warm colours and autumnal atmosphere of the backdrop bear upon the sitter with stern, symbolic force.

Two of the least comfortable pictures – *The Head of Medusa* (page 79) and *Despair* (page 81) – provide ominous background rumblings for the *Uneasy Portrait* (1978, page 98). The girl sits backed by these grisly companions, the Gorgon's head poised immediately above hers. That is suggested only, as the top frame of the *Portrait* crops the upper half of the background picture. To include the head would be 'playing to the gallery', a vulgarity which the portrait discreetly avoids.

The girl sits uneasily on her hard chair, which, elevated on a red-carpeted dais, edges her towards the viewer, towards an intimacy she would resist if she could. She wears leather boots, buttoned to within a few inches of the knee, and an elaborate dress with a high neck which tightly encircles her throat. Her hands are clasped nervously on her lap. The dress is dark blue and red, patterned with small leaf-like devices. The girl and her disconcerting sponsors behind are on harmonious artistic terms. Geometrical form determines both background and foreground, tone answers tone and a dominant red gives maximum emphasis to the girl's disquiet. Red flickers on the supporting *Medusa*, and the flesh tints of the girl are biliously sustained in the

**Uneasy Portrait (1978)**
*Oil on canvas, 30 × 25in (76.2 × 63.5cm),*
*private collection.*

**The Song of the Bird (c.1977)**
*Oil on canvas, 40 × 30in (101.6 × 76.2cm),*
*David Knox collection / Sotheby's, London.*

yellow ochres of *Despair* – the harmonics of a cohesive and powerful work. These large paintings, each so different in colour and tempo, are reconciled in the figure of the girl as agents of her disquiet.

The drawing of the face is sharp; the flesh is taut, the eyes are alarmed – characteristics of the highly strung. It is rightly considered one of Carel Weight's finest portraits.

The same young lady was the model for *Things of the Mind* (1979) – a portrait sensitive, introspective, with its look of guarded optimism in the diffident, expressive eyes.

*Captain Kitson and his Granddaughter, Linda* (1978, opposite) was Weight's response to a request from the granddaughter, a student at the RCA. (Later she served as an Official War Artist throughout the Falklands' conflict of 1982.) Her parents seem to have abandoned her when a child to the upbringing of grandparents. Her commission was of much urgency, as the old gentleman was close on a hundred and obviously near his end. And she adored him.

Mervyn Levy tells us that Weight was 'not greatly interested in the commissioned portrait'. But he warmed to the girl's childhood history – so like his own and his near-adoption by Rose – that his acceptance of her commission was immediate. Sadly, Kitson died two to three weeks after the work was completed.

Once at the Kitson's, Weight felt that he must include Linda in a double portrait which would juxtapose her youth to the Captain's age.

The old sailor – he had commanded a ship at Jutland – still obedient to the dictates of discipline, has dressed the shrunken body with customary care and sportingly in green, as if for a stroll in the country. The charm of life persists in the flourishes on the tiled surround of the fireplace, in the flowered chintz of the armchair and the rich oriental rug. The floor slopes forward to impel the subject upon the viewer's attention. The skin is drawn tightly over the bone; the eyes, with the paled vision of worn age, scan the past and future, very like Conrad's old Captain who, from 'his deep arm-chair . . . takes with untroubled mind the bearings for his last departure.'[9]

The two subjects are so placed that they are points on an axis. It runs obliquely from the left foreground – occupied by Kitson – to the top right corner where Linda sits. The two figures slip forward along the axis into the field of attention, separated, one from the other, by the maximum distance the room affords. The granddaughter's chair is green and harmonises with the old Captain's suit. She sits cross-legged, one hand in the pocket of her slacks, the other resting on her knee. She seems quite relaxed, her watchfulness withdrawn for the moment. He sits as easily as age allows in the heavy relaxation of the old. The interval between their chairs counterparts their dividing years. This geometric reference to the age gap underscores the tenderness of their relationship, which moves the artist to make his response. Between her easy, youthful pose and her grandfather's heavy and taut posture there exists, impalpably, the recognition of the reversal of their roles of guardianship.

Much tenderness here. It might be objected that the positive colours, the geometrical arrangement, the *estilo frio* would have more to do with the rationale of composition than with the sentiment of the subject. It is possibly a valid point. Weight's clear-sightedness informs his craftsmanship and controls any tendency towards the over-romantic.

Yet *The Song of the Bird* (c. 1977, left) appears to be exactly that – pure idyll, the substance of a madrigal. That is the immediate, superficial impression. A girl, graceful and slim in her light peach evening gown, stands listening to the bird. A young man, close by, is equally intent; he, too, is formally dressed. They are in the coign of a deep garden, walled, and with rich surrounding trees – and they are rapt and still like the hero and heroine of an Indian miniature listening for the Voice of the Thunder. The summer evening is indeed close, and the shadows are deepening – and foreboding. There is one who disturbs the stillness – a man leaving the garden, distressed and angry. Exposing his feelings to us, hugging them to himself, he clenches his right hand, and holds the other to his forehead. More than one of the deadly sins is abroad in the suburban bower meadow.

**Captain Kitson and his Granddaughter,**
**Linda (1978)**
*Oil on canvas, 36 × 28in (91.4 × 71.1cm),*
*Miss Linda Kitson / Royal Academy of Arts.*

# 9
# WEATHERS AND OTHER SUBJECTS
## The Later Style 1980–91

A downpour threatened our walk from the studio to the station. Heavy showers had fallen earlier, and I feared a soaking for us both. But he didn't seem concerned – prepared rather for any atmospheric interference which might, after all, provision his art. My impression is understandable. I was walking with one who dealt in atmospheres – quite as marvellously as Turner, according to the judgement of many.

Carel Weight's skies, ominously flushed, interpenetrate the human show as dramatically as Turner's. His two *Shipwrecks* are obvious examples. *The Presence* (page 110) remains Carel's finest atmospheric study where the interpenetration is every bit as obvious, though its function is more complex.

We must begin to read from the right. Here a blind man quietly comes forward, tapping with his white stick, and points the blindness of the sighted others to the glorious display spread out by the setting sun from pavement to zenith. The blind man and nature herself indict the incompetence of man's soul as quietly as the little dog repudiates his incapacity to perceive the supernatural!

> Think, at last
> I have not made this show purposelessly![1]

We were discussing *Before the Deluge* (1982). 'It was a good subject for me – not exactly original. Turner has a late picture which is rather similar. Everything is tensed-up. It's all about to happen.'

We spoke of the contrasting intensitives: the fiery, turbulent sky and the dull farmyard; the racing clouds and the long, heavily constructed wall; the shaken, writhing trees and the huge, firmly framed barns; the man 'staying put' on the far side of the midden – albeit with knocking knees – and the woman precipitately quitting the scene via the foreground.

The wall sets down an immensely powerful dynamic. Acutely angled at the corner, it is in crucial relationship with the gables of the two barns – a geometrical feature common to Carel Weight's dramatic subjects. The wall roots the attention to things terrestrial, the gables point to the sky.

The angled corner and the pile of midden against the wall insist upon the importance of the man – a reduced figure at the top of the yard. The woman, cropped to head and shoulders by the lower frame of the picture, hurries forward, her face in profile, upturned and agitated. It is skilfully animated – the woman coming on in blind haste, not looking where she is going, about to blunder into the spectator's stance. The commotion is opposed by the man. He is at a point of stasis which holds for the moment. But 'it's all about to happen.'

It is, in fact, all happening in *Jealousy* (c.1980, left), where the miserable weather is the image of the disordered human spirit. The slummy setting intensifies the sorry state of affairs that prevail. An embankment of masonry, its parapet slicing into the sky, carries the rail, with its arc-lamps, across a wet, inhospitable street. The structure is flanked by architectural monstrosities, reaching into the soggy clouds and indispensable to the overhead workings of the suburban permanent way. The sky, so cut about and restricted, sheds a faint flush on the shiny street.[2]

Here the daemon of jealousy, a Mephistophelean perversion of Cupid, aims his catapult at the chosen victim. She, a stony-faced woman in fur hat and blue coat, feigns indifference to the couple on the opposite pavement, locked in lascivious embrace. Two women look down from their bedroom windows, anxious to see how far the couple will take their love-making. Their intrusive curiosity adds chill to the slighted woman who does not turn to face the mockery of the daemon's generative organs, crudely and cruelly displayed.

Surely the mood's not quite so dark? Can we, in fact, take this daemon and his catapult more seriously than the arrow-discharging ladies and gentlemen in Cruikshank's *St Valentine's Day*?[3]

From the artist's bedroom we overlook the scene of *The Return* (1983, opposite), taking in part of the garden, his neighbour's lawn and an ugly Nissen-hut next door. The linear composition lifts in several parallel stages, transversely across the scene: the pathway where the hero stands, the trellissed wall, and the wall

**Jealousy (c.1980)**
*Oil on canvas, 60 × 48in (152.4 × 121.9cm), private collection.*

enclosing the neighbour's lawn and separating it from the Nissen, which structure puts a period to the ascending out-run of parallels, probes towards the drama in the foreground and introduces the roughly triangular complex of gloomy terraces against the sky.

'The sky,' said Carel Weight, 'is a bit uncertain. But you might take a chance with it.' Which the returning hero, uncertain of his welcome, has had to do.

He is tense, and everyone avoids him. Except the cloth-capped young man who seems to be ticking him off, while aggressively throwing a protecting arm across the girl's shoulders. Perhaps he's come to see his girl. Perhaps he's lost her. ('He's certainly lost something,' said Carel Weight.) An elderly couple – possibly the girl's parents – move away, down right. The hero stands, abject and shabby, at the apex of the human triangle. His hands droop cross-wise in front of him – an attitude taken from Flemish Masters (Petrus Christus, Dieric Bouts, van der Goes *inter alios*) to symbolise innocence. Here, repeated in the clasped hands of the two women, it denotes tension and relates to the triangularities of the composition. The elderly man raises a hand to his ear to increase the general edginess.

**The Return (1983)**
*Oil on canvas, 48 × 48in (122 × 122cm), private collection.*

The wide common is soaked and puddled (*After the Rains*, 1985).[4] It is calm. Puddles reflect the tints of passing clouds, or mirror brightly the cleared areas of sky. But for all that, the elderly folk out walking are pressing to leave with the apprehensive energy of age. They jostle out, crowding the left-hand corner of the picture. A young man accompanies an old lady, and looks impatient, as if tolerating with difficulty the needless solicitude of the old. Clearing skies had brought them out to enjoy their walk, but they cannot distinguish the signs that nature has relented and can now be trusted.

In *The Rains* (1980) five figures are in three groups, so dispersed as to leave the maximum space for the landscape. It is soaked and formidably spacious, nor is any shelter in sight. All are leaving the scene with anxious determination, except a man and a woman in the foreground who seem resigned to getting wet. The woman rests an arm on the man's shoulder, and looks questioningly into his blank, bewildered face. This is a tender, possibly a tragic undertone – unless, as in a study by Hiroshige,[5] the rain promises to be nothing more than a brief interference.

Now he simplifies his composition. Natural features are more expansively treated, the colours more intense. The stage is capacious, the number of accessories reduced but their scale is enlarged. Foliage is ponderous, in oppressive, Expressionist blobs.

*The Storm* and *The Wind*, both of 1991, make their impact through these big, startling effects. In earlier pictures, such as *The Moment* (page 61) and *The Presence* (page 110), trees and shrubs were plentiful and precisely represented. They were impassive onlookers, emanating atmosphere to deepen the stresses of the passing show. Or they were animated like a chorus, reflecting in their gestures and bearing the emotional crises of the human drama. Now they are formidable, assertive participants, as in *The Cricketer* (1984) and *The Phantom Monk* (1988).

The impact of *The Bag Snatcher* (1986) depends as much on the comment of the intrusive tree as on the crime itself. Its lumpy mass develops into a knob, like the Head of Medusa with tentacles flung out and sheared in the wind as if affected by the furore of the action.

In *The Wind* a strange natural object rears into the red sky. Not unlike the menacing form of Goya's *Gran Roca*[6] this shape is on an epic scale, like the Two Inseparables[7] in the Whirlwind of the *Inferno* – poised against, leaning into the sky. *The Rift* (1971) has a similar feature, and the scene, in general, resembles the setting of *The Wind* (1991).

Yet these later trends were anticipated as early as 1959 in, for example, *Sienese Landscape*, where trees are conventionally represented – with blobby foliage, even the bird-like shapes of *Evening Stroll* (1977) and *Land of the Birds* (1987–88, page 122).

*The Storm*, painted in 1991, employs an alarming *deus ex caelo* – a monstrous figure with short streaks of fiery hair. In true Gothic tradition, it swoops out of a dark wood with outspread, wing-like arms – a terrifying personification of the storm. The trees assume frightening shapes, the sky is smoked over with brown, strongly driven clouds.

Shadows become increasingly more vital to the atmosphere of these later works. In *The Phantom Monk* (1988, page 102) they creep across the broad green and penetrate the figure, engrossed in his ghostly missal. Black, clumsy arabesques, they image the baffled mind of the onlooking man – a cloddish individual who insensitively and unsuccessfully attempts to communicate with the monk, a poor ghost condemned to the earthbound study of his missal. The trees roar and whip in turmoil.

**The Phantom Monk (1988)**
*Oil on board, 48 × 36in (121.9 × 91.4cm),*
*Bernard Jacobson Gallery.*

The later world of Carel Weight has become *outré* and nightmarish, and its larger, open scale gives sufficient space for movement to evolve more emphatically. Shadows spread and shift, and deepen the sense of disquiet and discord, or – more quietly, as in *Winter Walk* (1987) – flex skeleton fingers on the grass and over the pedestrians themselves. The sinister effect is at its maximum in *Nightfall* (1984), intensified as it is by the notion of pursuit and menace, which devices are exploited again in *Guardian Angel* of the same year, and in *Bid for Freedom* (1985).

The setting is as much a living protagonist as the two lovers who, at the far right, stand in shocked surprise at the apparition of the *Primavera* (1988, opposite).[8] Each area of the picture contributes an essence of the season. An immense meadow, deep green with the maturing grain, shelves to the sky. Across this, on the far left, the Primavera moves, volatile, her hands outstretched in benediction. A narrow crescent of wild flowers, bordering the hem of the field, descends from the horizon to the nymph's feet – which do not touch the ground – and impels her flight from the scene. In a heavy counter-curve, the iron-spiked fence, enclosing the end of a grand garden, holds the lovers transfixed in their shock.

At their feet is a crescent-shaped mass of mixed daffodils and narcissi, bending in the wind of the northern spring. The man is an ungainly, dumpy fellow dressed for some rite – the morris dance, to judge from his flower-trimmed cap. His tabard-like jacket is boldly decorated with the face of the sun god, with its aureole of fiery locks. This emblem is repeated in the streaming gold hair of the Primavera and the sprays and branches of the garden, restless against the sky; a flock of birds scatters like leaves in the wind. Shadows shaped as sinister tongues probe from the garden to the meadow, lending further impetus to the flight of the nymph.

> As yet the trembling year is unconfirmed
> And winter oft, at eve, resumes the breeze.[9]

Anything portentous will, more often than not, provoke a mischievous interpretation. In discussing *Jealousy*, which also serves as *Envy*, the first of the *Seven Deadly Sins* (1979–80, page 104), Weight spoke of there being a 'good deal of Hogarth in it'.

The *Seven Deadly Sins* are executed in separate panels, arranged in cruciform pattern.[10] *Gluttony* and *Anger* are broadly farcical. In fact, *Anger* is taken to the excess of knockabout farce.

The hero, a slip of a lad, lays about him with a will and a chair. One of his victims – for there are two – sits at some distance, recovering his senses; the other topples in the foreground. The enraged youth is restrained in a side head-lock which an older man is applying, not too expertly. The chair still flourishes and the youth is eager to finish a job as yet only half-done.

It's not altogether a 'lark'. We can recognise the setting as one of those places too often associated with such goings-on. The design was originally used for *The Peacemakers*, one of the *Beatitudes* (page 70) in the Manchester Cathedral Mural, almost twenty years earlier.

In the fish-and-chip shop the glutton's immoderation has induced such discomfort as excites the interest of the queue and the man at the counter. He sits with loosened collar and, pausing between mouthfuls, awaits the relief of imminent eructation.

*Avarice*, *Lust* and *Sloth* form the crossbeam of the pattern. The central panel – at the meeting point of transom and vertical – is *Lust*. This rape scene – a girl is dragged into a red Austin 7 – is placed immediately above *Anger*. *Sloth* and *Avarice* – sins of the perverted love of self – are set isolated on the extremities of the crossbeam.

The latter is depicted as an unseemly Dormition, where the quiet of the death bed is violated by two rival claimants vigorously asserting their entitlement.

The slothful, drunken mother sleeps on as her child rushes into the room with her dress blazing. It is as powerful as any of Cruikshank's Temperance Cartoons – with the picture askew on the wall, and the can and empty bottle rolling on the floor.

The rape begins clumsily (*Lust*). The road slopes steeply against the efforts of the kerb-crawler as he strains to drag the girl into the car.

This cruciform arrangement demands a nicely managed colour orchestration. White is introduced via the lighted doorway and window in *Envy*, and predominates in the coverlet of the death bed in *Avarice*. It is sustained in the hoardings in *Anger*, and punctuates the glutton's plate and the chequered floor of the fish-and-chip shop. Yellow, blue and red relate in *Avarice* and *Sloth* at the extremities of the transom, and red appears throughout to associate all seven sins with the common evil of passion perverted. In the rape, both sky and

**Primavera** (1988)
*Oil on board, 48 × 48in (121.9 × 121.9cm),*
*private collection.*

**The Seven Deadly Sins (1979–80)**
*Oil on panels, on loan to the Tate Gallery*
*from the collection of J.R.M. Keatley.*
**Envy** *21 × 18in (53.5 × 45.7cm)*
**Avarice** *18 × 21in (45.7 × 53.5cm)*
**Lust** *18 × 18in (45.7 × 45.7cm)*
**Sloth** *18 × 21in (45.7 × 53.3cm)*
**Anger** *21 × 18in (53.3 × 45.7cm)*
**Gluttony** *21 × 18in (53.3 × 45.7cm)*
**Pride** *18 × 18in (45.7 × 45.7cm)*

car are red. Above stands the daemon of *Envy* in Mephistophelean hose. The facia of the fish-bar is scarlet, as is the dyspeptic glutton's face.

The series ends with *Pride*. A new Mini stands outside an end-of-terrace house. The brick façade is bright red, the little car a modest pink – a pale derivative of the proud, brilliant colour. A tall, over-dressed lady is about to put its capacity to the test.

The cruciform pattern is proof of serious intention – witness the ferocity of *Lust* and the Cruikshankian *Sloth*. Yet here – as in all Weight's religious themes – there is nothing sententious. Much of that is owing to the lively colours; more to the fantasy, satire and fun which tend towards the more venial shortcomings of ordinary life.

In Weight's transposition of *Susanna and the Elders* (1985, page 106) lofty seriousness disappears.

A strip of suburban parkland serves as the rich husband's garden. A door in the wall is being closed by a maid. Two old tramps, in the guise of the Elders, put their heads together to study Susanna as if connoisseurs of form, though poor Susanna's is sadly deficient of those curves which voluptuously and traditionally belong to her. A tubby, masculine figure, with stockings fallen around her flat-heeled, practical shoes, she stands on the low bank of a stream, looking down into the water. Here she is observed by some kind of waterfowl in a lighthearted allusion to the lubricious scrutiny of the Elders 'waxen old in wickedness'.

*Lot* (1982) has also 'waxen old', but not 'in wickedness'. That is the well-known preserve of his daughters. Hebrew thought of that time might well have approved Weight's interpretation. Some theologians consider the story an expression of the Israelites' hatred of the descendants of Lot's sons, born of his incestuous relationship with his daughters.

With his portable possessions in two big suitcases, he lumbers along on his way to the safety of Zoar. His wife stands massive and petrified, her face in clouds of flame and forever turned towards those places she was loath to leave. Her husband, 'vexed with the filthy conversation of the wicked', plods doggedly on. His daughters drag behind, more ponderously burdened with their plan for preserving the family from extinction.

More than 'conversation with the wicked' follows. Unfortunately, the scriptures are silent on the subject of Lot's vexation once he knows the cause of his daughters' pregnancies.

The *Crucifixion* of 1981 (page 107) is seen from some point behind Calvary, so that Weight is adopting the approach he exploited so successfully in the earlier epic version of 1959 (page 51). But now the viewpoint is advanced, and the cross is seen in close-up. A geometrical composition results in the four sections defined by its members. These are occupied by the crowd who, in their separate compartments, receive closer attention than they could be given in the other, more densely thronged version. There they served as supernumeraries to swell the scene and augment the drama of the tragic event.

This second *Crucifixion* is a far more intimate conception. An ornamental stream courses down from the left. Its surface reflects the head of the cross before bubbling turbulently out of the picture on the right. It is possible to distinguish the traditional actors at the foot of the cross. St Longinus wears a German helmet; Mary, with eyes closed, clasps her white hair; the Magdalen, in red, turns away as if bemused in her grief. A priest, in his dark clerical clothes, prays. Perhaps his presence is equivocal, as an exponent of the later sophistications of the Christian message. Near him, approaching the reflected image in the water, a young girl hurries forward. Her pleasant, open face looks up compassionately at the unseen figure, contrasting with the clergyman's professional anguish. On the opposite bank sit a young couple with hands clasped. They are intent yet surprised, as if puzzled by the event.

The two upper 'panels' are distinguished in various ways, yet the overriding impression is harmonious – of numerous individuals united in a shared experience on a piece of parkland or common familiar to them.

Brown streaks stain the back of both the vertical and the transom, and these have excited the curious to ask for an explanation. One enquirer suggested excrement – whether human or animal was not revealed. Mervyn Levy himself asked for an explanation, and Weight replied, 'I don't know,' then mentioned the excremental suggestion. Nothing further was said.

I venture this explanation: that the marks were merely a doodle[11] – the reverse of anything divinely inspired, or the result of even a brilliant idea. Anyway, an inclusion of this kind was bound to get the critics and art historians talking.

If something serious has to be said, then I would suggest that a passionate interest in a household – for instance, Helen Roeder's for old literature – could have entered its collective consciousness and returned an echo in Weight's subconscious mind as he worked.

**Susanna and the Elders (1985)**
*Oil on canvas, 72 × 22in (182.8 × 55.8cm),*
*Robin Bynoe collection.*

**106**

**Crucifixion II (1981)**
*Oil on panel, 84 × 44in (213.3 × 111.7cm),*
*Royal Academy of Arts Library/private*
*collection.*

107

Near the beginning of *The Vision of the Cross*, a poem much admired by Helen Roeder, the narrator declares himself unworthy of the vision:

*I stained with sins,*
*stricken with foulness: I saw the glorious Tree.*[12]

The original Old English carries the heavy alliterative stress, the force of the Anglo-Saxon intensitive, devices of rhetoric natural to the genius of the language. Could it be that the old scop's humility in approaching the sublime theme and which he expressed so forcibly might have moved the so-much-later visionary as he, in his turn, addressed the subject? And that his own unworthiness in the presence of the cross visibly sullies the cross itself?

I mentioned a little of this to Helen Roeder. But she could only agree that – knowing Carel's attitude to his work – it was more likely to be a 'doodle' than anything else.

It is never safe to apply generalisations, and what I have stated to be Weight's later style and later substance can only be accepted with caution. *Uneasy Scene* (1968) in the Royal College of Art, for example, might as easily belong to the eighties as to the sixties.

The vista is broad. A footpath, rough and broken, leads to the centre, to some enigmatic goal – a gloomy lake at the foot of dark mountains has been suggested. In the foreground are boldly painted, fraught individuals shaken by some distress whose source we cannot define. Shadows, similar to those we have seen in *The Phantom Monk* (page 102), lie across the pathway.

Carel Weight busies himself day after day, and his output is prodigious. Always there are new shocks to deliver, and gests and japes in profusion. The most recent work I was introduced to included *The Conflict between Children and Grown-Ups*. It was still on the stocks with the paint barely dry, and it generated much amusement. And I felt strongly the unpredictable nature of art: that the jokes had turned out, visually, not exactly as foreseen in the planning. 'I like my characters to run away with me.'

Hence, the impression that things had turned out other than expected, that the original plan had been modified in execution – that the characters had taken over. This phenomenon of the creative process, productive of the element of surprise, has much, if not everything, to do with the powers of arrest invested in Carel Weight's most successful work.

His awareness of the loneliness of man 'from his cradle' has perhaps become more oppressive. Some genre pieces may strike us that way. They are the winter scenes, such as *The Stone Hedge* (1983), *Blue Figure* (1985), *Winter Walk* (1987) and *Cold Day* (1988).

But the gloomy sense is relieved by the optimism of *Leaving the Town* (1980) and *Suburban Idyll* (1984). The first communicates the sense that the man and woman have long grown together into mature, mutual trust. In the second, the young couple exchange endearments amid the vegetable frames of an untidy allotment. The down-to-earth accessories of the setting underscore the nature of their love. From an elevated point, we overlook these lovers, and nothing is hidden. Theirs is an idyll of straight dealing and of love sufficient to face the open day.

# 10

## GHOSTS, CURIOSITIES AND THE
## SUBSTANCE OF NIGHTMARE

———————— • ————————

Had Mamillius been spared to tell his winter's tale, it would have been sad – about a man 'dwelt by a churchyard', such a one as might fit snugly into the world of Carel Weight.

I probed him on the occult, but he seemed to make light of the matter. His apparitions were figments of his imagination, no more. I questioned him on phobias – were there more than those he'd confessed to as childhood hauntings? Fire, for instance? No, nothing more than the common fear we all shared. It was not, and never had been, obsessive. He'd had his share of nightmares, of course – and a hair-raising spell on his own in a house in France which had a terrifying wartime history. Then I turned to Blake and how, as a child, he'd seen God peering in at the bedroom window – which 'set him a-screaming'.[1] Had Weight experienced such a starting point himself? Was any apparition foremost in his large spectral assembly? And the importunate questioner got what he deserved. 'Perhaps it would have been better for me,' said Weight, 'if I, too, like Blake, had seen God. But, no. Sadly enough, I've never seen the Lord!'

It was jocular, even dismissive. But recall what he told us about his *Crucifixion* of 1959 – how the agents of the sub-conscious were peremptory and, in their promptings, compelling. Carel Weight's haunted world becomes the thing it is on his submission to a force that 'strangely wills and works of itself'[2] and directs the artist's hand.

That is the essence of the creative process – the intervention of, the taking over by 'the magic hand of chance'. The more submissive the artist is to these complex promptings, the more convincing is the work of art which results. Where such submission is partial, then the work, however skilfully executed, will lack the integrity to convince.

If we consider *Natural History* (1963), then we face the difficulty of explaining away the queer lopped head so unaccountably holding the foreground. I was forced to ask if this were an afterthought. No – and Weight explained that it was as much part of the concept as the sinister birds pecking close by. I couldn't help feeling that both the head and birds had been dragged in forcibly, but for what purpose I could not imagine. Weight explained further: that the grotesques, which decorate the façade of the imposing building and stand sentinel on ridges and quoins, suggested the inclusion in the foreground of something startlingly gothic – hence, the head and the crows.

I am not sure about Weight's picture. The Natural History Museum depends for its effect on its immense proportions and not on the minutiae of its embellishments. It demands reportage, no more, and gains nothing from puzzling and fanciful variations. But it is in this genre that Carel Weight is supreme and seldom fails.

Speaking of his childhood, he has told us that for the lonely child to live in his imagination is to live with fears and terrors. In this respect, I have compared him with Wordsworth, and he himself has admitted to there being a Wordsworthian element in his work. Others have made frequent references to Goya, and I have often alluded to Blake.

Childhood was fraught with much that was frightening. The terrible Headmaster and Grandfather, the fire close to Rose's flat in Dawes Road, the racket of the first flying machines, the sights and sounds in the Fulham streets and parks during and after World War I, his parents watching a Zeppelin fall in flames out of the night sky. And besides, there's the child's delight in discovering sources of fear. Perhaps *Shadow People* (1976) derives from such a source. The setting is the one we encountered in *Barnes Station* (1976, page 95), but then it was Holy Ground, with crucifix on the parapet and a ghost-girl praying. Now, odd dusky shapes lurk here and there, or move furtively about. They could well originate from those shadow-shows we indulged in as children, when on walls or suspended sheets we vied in producing the most scary image.

Sinister *Caprichos* could originate from such sources. But Weight's *Caprichos* are not like Goya's. They do not emanate from a crippled mind and demand exposure as psychological therapy. *Nightmare* (1991, page 120) is an exception.

**The Presence (1955)**
*Oil on canvas, 47½ × 80in (120.7 × 203.2cm), Royal Academy of Arts Library / private collection.*

It exploits the idea of entrapment and derives from Weight's military service. He was required for guard duty, but was ill and exposure to the weather was dangerous. But he pleaded his condition in vain. He was trapped in the rigours of the regulations by the adamantine deafness of the enforcing officer. His hopeless situation assumes the image of being caught in the path of a train from which there is no escape. Sheer walls – one slaty-grey, the other of scarlet brick – plunge down in an artificial gorge which guides the rails to the tunnel mouth. From here the train emerges. The sides of the gorge press the rails so close as to leave no margin of refuge. This allegory of the original event, appearing fifty years later, proves the persistent nature of its haunting. It accounts for numerous variations on the theme of pursuit and frustrated escape.

But as for 'therapy': I am very sure Carel Weight would deny that *Nightmare*, or any of the 'numerous variations' had much, if anything, to do with the notion of therapy. They were good subjects for his art, and it is unlikely that he would allow more than that.

M.R. James, as a leading authority in the genre of ghostly narrative, writes in his Introduction to V.H. Collins' *Ghosts and Marvels*:

> Two ingredients most valuable in the concocting of a ghost story are, to me, the atmosphere and the nicely managed crescendo.

Atmosphere is, in fact, the chief ingredient of Weight's narrative. The 'crescendo', the build-up to the climax, the stages that lead the attention to the central event, may at times be obvious as, for example, in *Nightmare*. The train's sonorous approach from the tunnel mouth, the down-swept walls, the gleaming rails between – all point to the trapped figures scattering in panic from the track.

The crescendo is more 'nicely managed' in *The Moment* (1955, page 61), where the dynamics are quieter. An onlooking figure, an on-thrusting wall, and lines of pavement and road carry the eye hastily along to the central, imminent disaster. Here again is the theme of entrapment. It moves to no such clangorous climax as

*Nightmare* but, in its quieter way, is equally horrifying. The poor girl, in the blind fear of ineffectual flight, blunders into the path of some inevitable disaster.

In *The Presence*, also of 1955 (left), the crescendo is over and the finale to which it has led is resounding in a powerful discord. The blazing sky and the patterning trees against the fiery cyclorama are in counterpoint to the undertones of the suburban street, indifferent to the strident magnificence of the sunset. There we see: a woman, short-sleeved and anxious to get home; gossips stopped to chat on things other than nature; a cyclist concerned to ride off; a blind man fumbling his way to the kerb as the image of the general indifference. Maybe the discord is partially resolved in the perceptiveness of the little dog. He alone sees the *Presence* – his master is half-asleep on the bench – and perhaps has felt more profoundly than his superiors the glorious commonplace of his evening walk!

That slight commentary may be enough to alert the reader to this aspect of Weight's composition, to a music which can be tragic and plaintive, macabre: jauntily so, at times, and – at others – full of shrill alarm.

Numerous stimuli act powerfully on the romantic temperament, none more so than the past, and again I canvass support from the expert Dr James:

> For the ghost story a slight haze of distance is desirable. 'Thirty years ago,' 'Not long
> before the war,' are very proper openings.[3]

Weight has two ghosts, at least, dressed in a style remote from the present – the child in *Barnes Station* (page 95) and the eponymous heroine of *The Presence*. As a rule, his early apparitions are clearly focused, the later more frequently in the approved 'haze' – although their tendency is to irrupt into the foreground with considerable violence.

Weight is master of the loaded atmosphere, as we have seen. The *Battersea Medusa* (1974–75, right) evokes an atmosphere of extreme disquiet. Can it be that the masks in Messrs Cavalcade's window, with their crude, far-distant relationship to classical drama, have conjured the Medusa to appear in that drab street? Masks – frozen simulacra of the living face – are disquieting things. Witness the use of them by Goya in *The Burial of the Sardine* (1793), in the *Caprichos Nadie se conoce* and *Sueño de la mentira y la ynconstancia*. In his Second Madrid Album *Mascaras Crueles* speak for themselves.

*Trying on Masks* (1972, page 112) – relying for its effect on weird juxtapositions and appearances – is the quintessential study of masks which aim to terrify.

The Medusa has left the scene, we've crossed the road, and are now outside Messrs Cavalcade – a near-relation to the Ostend shop run by Ensor's parents, also stockists of carnival paraphernalia.

> I never, ever, actually saw anyone in the shop, except on one occasion when I saw a
> filthy old woman come out wheeling a pram full of parcels. I have no idea what it all
> meant, but it was strange. The memory continues to haunt me.[4]

But now two figures have come out, a disconcertingly rigid couple who pause outside the windows. In one a female effigy is masked in a grotesque parody of feminine charm with round, glassy eyes and arch, inane smile. She holds a Union Jack – a monstrous, ironic comment on patriotism. The two customers are about to don their purchases. One has favoured a bleeding skull whose mouth is a sagging crescent of blood. The other, whose features are so pasty he could already be masked, has chosen a head, half-tiger, half-human, with eyes of evil intent, teeth dreadfully crowded. These two ugly, androgynous customers have shopped successfully for masks even uglier than themselves. In short, it's a real fright, and I am forced to wonder what reaction it evokes from its owner!

But when all's said and done, we come back to Carel Weight's admission 'I have no idea what it all meant. But it was strange.' But he won't stop at that, and goes on, 'When, years later, I decided to paint the street and the shop, I wanted to intensify the sensation of strangeness and introduce into the picture some horrifying note. So I brought in the Medusa.'

She comes towards us with her snood of snakes, spurts of fire issuing from their jaws – an image of our innermost terrors openly displayed. A few people pass by in the background; they see nothing to render their street remarkable. Nor are they the Medusa's concern – it is we she singles out. And if we turn back to Chapter 1 we shall find Carel Weight expressly stating the function of this vision:

**The Battersea Medusa (1974–75)**
*Oil on panel, 36 × 28in (91.4 × 71.1cm),*
*Arts Council Collection, The South Bank*
*Centre, London.*

**The Witches are Here (1984)**
*Oil on canvas, 83 × 44½in (211 × 113cm),
Saatchi Collection, London.*

**'I too was here when I was young' (1988)**
*Oil on canvas, 50 × 36in (127 × 91.4cm),
Jeffrey and Catherine Horwood collection.*

**Votive Picture (1972)**
*Oil on panel, 27 × 68in (68.5 × 172.7cm),*
*Mr and Mrs Alfred Mignano collection.*

The symbolism of the snakes, still vigorously writhing, keeps alive the buried horror of these two awful people.

It need not divert us from what we know so well of Carel Weight – his readiness to smile at anything pompous and over-serious.

'*I too was here when I was young*' (1988, page 113) is pure whimsy, but Weight's ghosts are more in earnest than his witches. As part of experience, they are urgent in their appeal – wistful or admonitory – and we must attend. The witches could be out of some old drollery – pantomime creatures who bungle their spells, or ineptly manage their broomsticks.

In one instance they're brought on the scene by a whim stimulated by – of all holy objects – a church steeple! 'You see,' said Carel Weight, 'it does look like a witch's hat, and that's how they come to be hovering round the church.'

The picture is *The Crossing* (1972), where the witch who is first on the scene floats on her broom over the churchyard, while looking down at the boys on the crossing. At the same time, she displays an immodest length of leg from under her cutty-sark.[5] It seems like a pointed gesture aimed at the boys, although they have their backs to the entertainment offered them *gratis* (?) by the Prince of the Powers. Their facial expressions would suggest a sort of guilt, but in this genre the narrative is not explicit – nor should it be.

It is not safe to dismiss occult phenomena lightly. The purpose of *The Crossing* was to entertain. But the subject may have something essentially to do with puberty – a common nexus between the rational and occult phenomena. And perhaps the churchy setting enjoins us to adopt some measure of seriousness in our appreciation.

Weight found a happy subject in *The Witches are Here* (1984, page 2 and page 113).[6] Pattern and powerfully contrasting colours, spirited action above and below are compositional details of a work, good humoured, indeed almost farcically inclined. And yet – a woman in slacks stops, utterly bewildered. Witches – quite a posse of them – plunge down in V-formation and scatter a bunch of kids in a like V-shaped pattern. The woman in slacks wonders what the deuce can be going on for, as yet, the witches are outside her orbit of vision – which could be limited in any case, to judge from the vacancy of her expression. Have the children got their comeuppance? Have they been dabbling in diableries? A boy's crash helmet displays the skull-and-crossbones, the others are masked, and all scurry away from those who need no masks to terrify.

All the witches wear comfy-looking carpet slippers – those of the flight leader are red and capacious. Another sports red-and-white striped stockings. Nothing wrong with that. A third, inexpert, with arms rigid on her broom, is more preoccupied with riding techniques than with hunting children. A sense of duty impels the leader to set an example. Bearing down on the girl, she chases her across the road, open-mouthed to utter some horrifying cry.

**Disaster at the Royal Academy Dinner 1958 (1982)** *Drawing.*

If we must look for a nexus, then the girl is the likeliest candidate. Or, perhaps the most innocent person present – the woman in the slacks who wonders what it's all about?

It matters so little as we increasingly appreciate the composition for its own sake – its colour and pattern; the action, offsetting the static block of the house, in buoyant flight above and precipitate flight below – repose and fluidity poised and balanced.

The irruption of an unexpected event into the banal mould of ordinary life galvanises it with dramatic tension. 'You stand a chance of catching the attention,' said Weight, 'if in a very realistic picture, you can get away with a piece of fantasy.' This happens with a vengeance in *Votive Picture* (1972, page 114). The scene is Dawes Road, Fulham, where Rose had her flat and where Carel Weight spent most of his early life. He could capture the flavour of the place at a stroke. A complex junction of roads of sweeping curves and counter-curves adapts well to the agitated scene.

The format is a polyptych of four panels derived from votive pictures in Italy. The first two panels are full of rush and frenzy, in sharp contrast to the calm indifference of the third. Here, at the edge of the curb an elderly, soldierly man stands rigid, almost to attention. He looks away to his left as if something more absorbing is going on outside the picture.[7] Two respectable spinsters move sedately from the scene, equally unconcerned. And there's plenty to concern them.

For a murder has been committed in the first panel. It is overlooked by the apparition of the Virgin in a shop window in a gleaming mandorla from which she inclines compassionately towards the body, slumped across pavement and curb. It awakens a variety of responses. A young woman takes to her heels, momentarily sheltered by a man who, slow on the uptake, is sluggishly beginning to realise what has happened.

It prompts numerous questions, of course. Each individual viewer will find solutions to his own satisfaction, and each will realise how little any 'solution' matters. In disturbing the viewer, it achieves its aim.

**Sunshine and Shadow (c.1968)**
*Oil on panel, 21 × 13in (53.3 × 33cm),*
*Mr and Mrs Alfred Mignano collection.*

In composition the work is masterly. A 'falling action', a *diminuendo*, if you like, is punctuated by a series of different reactions, some of which are low-keyed, others at fever pitch. Thus, from the climax – the murder – on the far left, the *diminuendo* is confused in its passage to the *termino*, which is baffled as the turbulent theme requires. The cyclist, whom we see through Messrs Batchelors' window, leaves, presumably deaf to, unaware of, what has happened. In the window above Batchelors' facia a woman leans out at full stretch – all agog with excitement – while below the man stands to attention and the unflurried spinsters walk calmly away. It is a Carel touch *par excellence*. A woman is distraught, another registers shock, a dog goes out on its doggy way without giving the matter another thought. It is an unending source of fascination.

He explained the origin of this picture:

> In Italy I was struck by the votive pictures in the churches. If someone had escaped
> from some serious situation, or danger, he could have the crisis represented in a
> painting, a votive picture, to remind him of God's mercy, and of his obligation to be
> grateful.

Weight's picture of a murder admonishes the criminal to be constantly penitent.

Dawes Road was also the setting for *Day of Doom* (page 69) – both pictures were completed in 1972. The cyclist, seen through the window of Batchelors' corner shop, is common to both. The two appearances indicate her importance. In *Votive Picture* she represents a common attitude of not wanting to get involved. In *Day of Doom* her significance can scarcely be overstated, as typifying the whole condition of man in the Ultimate Crisis (see page 69).

In Carel Weight's store cupboard of effects, we should inventory the following. The Unexpected Presence; the *Doppelgänger*; The Element of Espial; The Unrevealed Source of Fear; Animism; The Thwarted, or Doomed Effort to Escape, and – closely associated – The Absence of Refuge. But we must never overlook The Liberal Tincture of Humour. Note his delightful record of the *Disaster at the Royal Academy Dinner* of 1958 (a sketch done in 1982; page 115).

An unexplained presence, or one of dubious function, intensifies the atmosphere in *Her Brother's Ghost* (1960). At the back of a deep garden, where light and dark merge and conflict, a statue looks towards the action, a solitary, detached witness. Yew trees cover the background, the boughs of one sweeping over the statue like an immense wing. Here, you feel, much could happen, that it was here the girl looked at the flowers and the ghost appeared. It's quite a sunny spot, its concentrate in the greenery and scattered flowers. Light slants on to the path and runs up to the ghost and the frightened girl. Stopping her ears against his cry, she rushes out, hair flying and with troubled face.

A second path allows another possibility – that the girl, visiting the outhouses on this side, was not pursued but ambushed. It could be a childish prank, but if not – what can be the score he has to settle?

M.R. James has further advice for authors of ghost stories:

> It is not amiss sometimes to leave a loophole for a natural explanation; but I would say,
> let the loophole be so narrow as not to be quite practicable.[8]

There is no loophole for natural explanations in *Sunshine and Shadow* (c.1968, left). The presences here – and there are three – function mysteriously. Indeed, that could well be their role – as intelligences in an old mystery or morality. The woman is a tragic figure, moving to a sunlit garden, bearing her incubus on her back – a skeleton, open-chapped, hideously grinning. She has emerged from deep shadows, the sunlit garden beckons, and she is about to step on to the bricked garden path, enriched by flowers in a border that runs its whole length. The other side is a wild area of vague shadows and tangled, umbrageous growths. Here an obscure, androgynous figure stands motionless, draped in black from head to foot. It seems intent on the statue, modestly screened, in the flowered border. It savours of espial and the dark figure could represent one or other of the vices.

Even more mysterious is the woman's wan smile directed at us. She has little cause for this, locked as she is in grisly, burdensome arms. And yet she smiles as if in a morality, inviting us to reflect.

Espial, as Weight exploits it, is a powerful dramatic instrument. Munch was its great exponent. Weight's watchful houses are not as overtly malign as Munch's: perhaps it was extravagant of one critic to declare that they seemed 'on the brink of a nervous breakdown.'[9]

**Foxwood (1968)**
*Oil on canvas, 36 × 39in (91.4 × 99cm),*
*John Brandler collection / Saatchi Collection*
*Library.*

**The Flying Machine (1982)**
*Oil on panel, 5 × 15in (12.7 × 38cm),*
*Robin Bynoe collection, London.*

There's a detached house [said Weight], and there's a narrow alleyway each side and I've often thought of sinister things appearing along that avenue. And what better than some flying witches?[10]

All that can be said of Weight's houses is that they register indifference, or they're unlikely venues for witches. An exception is *Young People in a Landscape, Grantchester* (1988), where observing windows peer from between trees with an air of malevolent curiosity.

Yews, trained into the shapes of birds, brood over a wild outlandish scene in *Land of the Birds* (1987–88, page 122).[11] *The Evening Stroll* (1977) and *The Watcher* (1991) exploit the same brooding shapes atop the hedgerow to preside over human relations tense and stretched to breaking point.

Walls, inanimate things, animate trees – hug-secret[12] or threatening – figures in his own paintings are agents of Weight's artistic espial. Apparitions overlook, or are themselves observed by, intuitively perceptive dogs.

In some cases the springs of disquiet can only be guessed. What is it about *Foxwood* (1968, page 117), for example, that causes such panic haste, such apprehension in the upward glance, such a stopping of the ears? Does a passing jet reawaken childhood fears, or rattle the windows of *Foxwood* like some fractious household ghost? Or does the next-door shrubbery, tipped with orange, reassert the child's fear of fire?

The dark hut must hold the secret of *The Invocation* (1976). What or whom is invoked by the wild, distraught figure that rushes towards us? Is it a wilderness from which he demands relief? Has the hut any bearing on his flight? Have the two gates, impediments to escape, merely delayed the realisation that the wilderness is himself, that the dark restrictions of the hut are his own limitations from which there is no escape?

Carel Weight explains how he was walking once in the Sussex countryside when a terrible cry pierced the quiet. A long tenseness ensued, prompting the vision to be realised later as *The Invocation*.

A lighter method is exploited in the notions of ascent and descent which we have already seen in *The Assumption of the Virgin* (1972, page 90). The two aeroplanes of *The Amazing Aeronaut* (1933, page 23) and the much later *The Flying Machine* (1982, above) – splendidly unpractical – terrified him when a child with their down-to-earth flight and awful noise. His two infant fears – the timber-yard fire and the early flying machines – account for the aerial sources of alarm in so many of his picture.

We have a delightfully comic mixture of humour and alarm in *The Invasion* (1987–88, page 119) where the invading troops descend – rather like Bosch's Falling Angels – in a motley array of guises and disguises: clowns, bandsmen, a dog, a cat on hind legs and equipped with shears. A drummer brings up queer reserves who float over the dark hedgerow. Somehow they are less innocent than Chagall's troupes. The very ordinary lanes, overlooked by redbrick dwelling houses, have become suddenly no place like home, as two hefty lads make a bolt for it.

**The Invasion (1987–88)**
*Oil on canvas, 48 × 60in (121.9 × 152.4cm),*
*Saatchi Collection, London.*

Wholly amusing is the affectionate picture of Weight's favourite Uncle Percy as the conjuror in *The Masterstroke of Dr Tarbusch* (1960, page 120). The magician demonstrates his control over gravity by sending skyward over the roof of the Variety Theatre – too restricted for all his miraculous creatures – an assorted collection of marvels. These include an alligator of pre-history, a fish straight out of Bosch, a witch on her broomstick, a

Lion and woman and the Lord knows what.[13]

Fear comes from some hidden source in *Frightened Children* (1981). Their pursuer is unseen, but he'll be as fleet-footed as his quarry is leaden-limbed. It is, indeed, the common substance of nightmare – the hopeless flight, the imminent capture. Or there is no clear escape route. Or it's obstructed. And should a hiding place offer, then it's more likely than not to play false.

In flight from an ill-intentioned youth, a small girl rushes pell-mell down *The Causeway* (1983, page 120). It is narrow, slatted and angled as if to throw drags on the girl's efforts to escape, to keep her within range of her pursuer. The causeway itself is sited in an ill-defined region of turbulent water, lofty sinister trees and

**The Masterstroke of Dr Tarbusch (1960)**
*Oil on panel, 36 × 20in (91.4 × 50.8cm),*
*private collection.*

**The Causeway (1983)**
*Oil on canvas, 65 × 65in (165.1 × 165.1cm),*
*Lord Gowrie collection.*

**The Dream (1986)**
*Oil on canvas, 56 × 56in (142.2 × 142.2cm),*
*Saatchi Collection, London.*

plunging earth. It is partly railed, but at the angle a gap seems to give access to an expanse of open downland. Her position is precarious, the escape route treacherous, and capture is imminent. It is a bridge over chaos, across which her straining legs struggle heavily. Her scared eyes suggest she has looked back to see her persecutor, set in cruel purpose, heave at the rails and launch himself into stronger pursuit.

Of deeper importance to Carel Weight is the enclosed state of psychological entrapment. Some notable examples are *The Silence* (1965, page 83), *The World We Live In* (1970–73, page 89), *Despair* (1969, page 81) and *Mrs Rochester* (1973, see page 92). The last two are such powerfully haunting works they could not have been painted without a profound understanding of dejection, and compassion for those isolated and trapped in their derangement of mind. They are executed in sombre tones – the poor seated man the very epitome of *Despair*; inner corrosion worrying away the soul of the confused unhappy woman.

The more recent *Nightmare* (1991, page 120) has been mentioned already, but requires closer consideration.

Two are caught – a young workman and a girl – in the path of an approaching train. Its lamp shows a single, sinister gleam in the tunnel as it emerges into a narrow strait between high flanking walls. One is in cut-blocks of thunderous grey, the other in brilliant scarlet bricks. The track is electrified, its three rails thrusting towards our own position as spectators. On the tunnel-head is a bowler-hatted man who peers over the parapet, horrified by the imminent catastrophe. Behind him a church spire cuts into the purple drape of the sky – a narrative undertone and crucially important to the tapering dynamics of the composition. Two windows in the grey wall on the right overlook the scene and glow pallidly as if lighted by an incipient fire within. A face appears at one, impassive, indifferent to the terror-stricken couple who scatter from the tracks to the dubious refuge at the sides. In her mad scramble the girl's upraised leg is perilously close to the central, power-bearing rail. It is the extreme, the 'classic' example of spiritual entrapment expressed in starkly physical terms. The paint is strident to accord with the train's sonorous approach and the wild panic in the cutting.

Stridency of this kind reinforces the terror inspired by *The Cricketer* (1984). Blackened stems support a frieze of blazing leaves between a densely blue sky and acid-green grass. Near the front, yellowing trunks throw out stripped, gesturing branches. The Cricketer's gear matches the strong blue and blacks. He comes away grimly from the terror he has caused, dark face expressionless and cruel. Her red sleeves extended, a mother gathers her frightened child into a strong, comforting embrace. And we are left guessing again – finding and rejecting interpretations, as usual.

Weight's powers to involve, to stimulate his viewers may be briefly summarised.

A character rushes towards us – indeed, rushes us. Incongruities engage us everywhere. As spectators we are drawn into the *mise-en-scène* via some material route like a 'shared access'. The same device holds our attention fixed on the murderous figure stalking towards the red archway in *The Dream* (1986, page 121). Always we are involved, always hurried from one emotion to another.

There is tragedy, too, besides the fun, terror and creepy things we have looked at in this chapter. *The Blind Boy* (1984, opposite) is closely wrapped against the intrusion of the rowdy fun promised by the pop festival band. In flamboyant, disconcerting get-ups they pass, wholly absorbed in their racket. A drugged girl has flopped against the wall and covers an ear against the din and, dismissive of her gift of sight, turns from the outrageous musicians. She points and relieves the tragedy at one and the same time. Significant supernumeraries of this sort are many and various.

Imponderables arrest the attention and they are general. *Land of the Birds* (1987–88, left) is almost as mystifying as Bosch's *Garden*. Whatever are these unlikely riverside buildings in lurid red and yellow over which the bird-shaped trees preside? It is the substance of a dream, an outlandish Gothic setting with characters to match, preoccupied with their several curious concerns. The masses are immense and simplified and vigorously coloured. It is a favoured rhetoric of powerful, direct emphases sufficient to deliver the intended, physical shock. It is best to have these out into the open and get used to them.

'I am getting much more interested in colours,' said Carel Weight. 'The whole modern idea is that one designs in colours.'

At the time I am writing Carel Weight is in his eighty-sixth year, and his stature is of enlarged inventiveness. His powers of arrest have increased with the dynamism of his latest images, and his Palace of Varieties is as well-stocked as ever.

By its very nature, the analytical monograph risks losing sight of the rarer visionary expression. But if it indicates a little of what we should expect from a picture by Carel Weight, it will have served its purpose.

**Land of the Birds (1987–88)**
*Oil on board, 48 × 36in (121.9 × 91.4cm),*
*Bernard Jacobson Gallery, London.*

# NOTES

## 1 AFFINITIES, AVERSIONS AND ART – NARRATIVE AND VISIONARY

1 Catalogue of *An Eightieth Birthday Tribute* (Mervyn Levy), an exhibition presented by Friends of the Royal Academy.
2 Mervyn Levy, *Carel Weight* (Weidenfeld and Nicolson, 1986).
3 Levy: op. cit.
4 Ibid.
5 Artist's Note in the catalogue of the *Exhibition of New Paintings* to celebrate his retirement as Professor of the Painting School, Royal College of Art. Leonie Jonleigh Studio, Wonersh, Guildford, 1973.
6 Levy: op. cit.
7 Ibid.
8 Carel Weight to George Weight, a family genealogist (22 November 1985).
9 Peter Crookson: *Sunday Times Magazine* 4 June 1989.
10 Levy: op. cit.
11 Carel Weight: 'The Way I Work: A Statement by the Artist', *The Painter and Sculptor* Spring 1962, Vol IV, No IV.
12 Ian Simpson: *The Artist* September 1983.
13 The text is as follows (14 December 1969):

> *The Enraged Musician*. Painted in 1931. It was my first picture painted as a student at Goldsmith's College at a time I was particularly interested in classical mural painting (Piero della Francesca and Botticelli). The picture has a number of references to things I was then thinking of and to my childhood, my family and friends – it is probably the most personal picture I ever painted.
>
> Reading from the left – the man at the window is Cézanne and the woman with the cockney hat is my mother. The house behind was once in Cary Street where my grandfather lived (the door of which is in the Victoria and Albert Museum), the artist painting by the railings was one of my art teachers at Goldsmith's, John Mansbridge. Both the man collecting and the figure next to him playing the accordion were based on myself. The statue is another friend Paul Drury an etcher, and the dwarf with the trombone a fellow student. The bearded man and the lady with the shopping bag are brother and sister who both played an important part in my childhood – particularly the latter who was my foster mother. The enraged musician himself is my painting master James Bateman later RA. The dog was from a stuffed dog in the Natural History Museum.
>
> The idea of the picture came from the sketch from Hogarth of the same subject treated in quite a different manner.
>
> The picture was painted with a completely new ground of titanium white* which was only just beginning to be used at that time. True to the traditional method the whole underpainting was done in terra vert and the colour was added with a wax medium diluted with turpentine.

The picture was first exhibited at the Royal Academy in 1932.

*Titanium white: A fine, very durable pigment first manufactured as an artist's material c1920. Weight was introduced to it some ten years later by an early manufacturer. He has used it ever since.
14 Keith Roberts: *Burlington Magazine* May 1968.
15 Jane Stroud: 'Gallery Focus', *The Artist* November 1988.
16 Mervyn Levy: *An Eightieth Birthday Tribute*. Op. cit.
17 Wordsworth: *The Prelude* X, 81–2.
18 Levy: *Carel Weight* (1986). Op. cit.
19 Carel Weight: 'The Way I Work'. Op. cit.
20 Ibid.
21 Catalogue of the *Retrospective Exhibition*, Royal Academy, 1982. Carel Weight in conversation with Norman Rosenthal, Director of Exhibitions.
22 Grey Gowrie in *Modern Painters A Quarterly of the Fine Arts*, Vol. 1 No. 3, Autumn 1988 (Fine Arts Journals Ltd).
23 William Blake: *A Descriptive Catalogue* 1808. *Ruth – A Drawing*.
24 Horace Shipp in *Apollo* May 1959.

## 2 PORTRAITS – A CHANGE OF DIRECTION

1 Wordsworth: *Lines Composed above Tintern Abbey* (1798).
2 Conversation with Norman Rosenthal. Op. cit.
3 See Mervyn Levy: *Carel Weight*. Op. cit.
4 Ibid.
5 Edward Thomas, *Cock-Crow* (1936) Faber & Faber.
6 Thomas Hardy: 'I look into my glass' *Wessex Poems* (1898).
7 See Fragonard's *L'Amant Couronné, ou Devant le Peintre* (c1770), Frick Collection, New York.
8 This wood sculpture is now in the Michael C. Rockefeller Wing of the Metropolitan Museum, New York.
9 Hogarth (1697–1764): *Analysis of Beauty* – Chapter X: 'Of Composition with the Serpentine Line' (rejected passage), 1753.
10 Edna Ellen McKeown (before her marriage) was born in Belfast in 1900. She was educated at Roedean, where she became Head of School, before proceeding to Newnham College, Cambridge, to take the Law Tripos. Afterwards she was a law student at the Inner Temple and later Assistant Editor of the magazine *The Queen*. An Irish Hockey International, she was capped twice in 1923. Both events were unfortunate for Ireland, losing to England at Dublin (0–3), and to Wales at Colwyn Bay (2–4).

11 Thomas Hardy: *In Time of 'The Breaking of Nations'*.

## 3 EXPERIENCE OF WORLD WAR II

Details of Weight's life in the ranks are taken from the artist's private letters to Miss Roeder. His work abroad as Official War Artist is documented in further letters to Miss Roeder, published as *The Curious Captain* (Camberwell Press, 1989). Miss Roeder herself edited. Other material is in the Archives of the Imperial War Museum, London.

1 *The Studio*, which praised the Artists' International Association's enterprise in arranging the exhibition, reproduced Weight's *It Happened to Us*. 'The exhibition has proved a great success. All day long the little gallery was crowded with just the kind of people that in normal circumstances have never any opportunity of seeing actual paintings.' Jan Gordon's London Commentary in *The Studio* Vol 122, December 1941

2 Imperial War Museum Archives, file GP/55/156 (Carel Weight), Second World War Archive.

3 Weight's war service may be summarised thus:

1942:     In the Training Centre (RAC), Warminster, Wilts.
*Transferred:* Driving and Mechanical Wing (RAC), Catterick, North Yorkshire.

1943:     *Transferred:* Royal Engineers (Survey Section – Draughtsmen and Topographical Dept), Wynnstay Hall, Ruabon, near Wrexham, North Wales.
*Transferred:* Royal Army Education Corps, Command College, London, as Sergeant i/c Art Department.

1945–6:   Appointed Official War Artist with the rank of Captain. Active in Italy, Austria and Greece.

4 Lionel Brett succeeded to the Peerage as Lord Esher in 1963, and followed Sir Robin Darwin as Rector and Vice-Provost of The Royal College of Art (1971–78). He was a distinguished architect and was responsible for numerous national projects, including the planning of the post-war New Towns.

5 Miss Roeder believed that this second, more considerate posting was authorised in the mistaken belief that as Carel Weight was an artist he was necessarily an expert cartographer.

6 See Ian Hay: *The Story of the Royal Ordnance Factories 1939–1948* HMSO 1949 and *The Hereford Times* 13 January 1945, p 7.

7 See headnote Chapter 3.

8 The picture is reproduced in *The Curious Captain*.

9 Imperial War Museum Archives.

10 Michael Rooney, RA – Carel Weight's former pupil – in his Introduction to *An Eightieth Birthday Celebration*, the catalogue of the touring exhibition organised by the Hastings Museum and Art Gallery with assistance from the Brandler Galleries, Brentwood (1988–89).

11 Byron: *Don Juan*

12 Imperial War Museum Archives.

13 Browning: *Two in the Campagna* (*Men and Women*) 1855.

## 4 THE POST-WAR PERIOD

1 Ron Kitaj, a 'Pop' artist. He was American and a 'significant influence' on David Hockney.

2 Derek Boshier, another 'Pop' artist.

3 Michael Rooney: Introduction to the catalogue of the touring exhibition *An Eightieth Birthday Celebration*, organised by the Hastings Museum of Art and the Brandler Galleries, Brentwood.

4 Michael Rooney, op. cit.

5 Quoted in Professor Christopher Frayling: *The Royal College of Art: 150 Years of Art and Design*. (Barrie and Jenkins, 1987).

6 See Edmund Blunden: *Undertones of War* Chapter XIV. (R. Cobden-Sanderson Ltd, 1928).

7 The Franz-Josef Bridge over the Moldau at Prague (1868), designed by the same engineer, R.W. Ordish (1824–88).

8 Carel Weight quoted by G.S. Sandilands in *The Artist* August 1959.

9 I have been unable to trace this work, so that the comparison with *Veronese Night* may not be as close as I've assumed.

10 Marlowe: *Dr Faustus* Scene XVI.
See Carel Weight: *The Artist* June 1956.
Stanley Spencer greatly admired *The Betrayal*, speaking of it with the enthusiasm he reserved exclusively for his own work. He pointed out the skill with which Weight had assembled all the details given in St Mark's Gospel.

He waxed enthusiastic about the picture as a whole. I was surprised and delighted. Because, although he'd talk eloquently about his own pictures, I'd never heard him talk about anyone else's!

(Weight in conversation, 31 November 1992)

## 5 SURREALISM AND THE CONVERSATION PIECE

1 Conversation with Norman Rosenthal in the catalogue of the RA Retrospective Exhibition, 1982. Op. cit.

2 Mervyn Levy: *Carel Weight*. Op. cit.

3 Walt Whitman: 'As I Ebb'd with the Ocean of Life' *Sea-Drift* (1860).

4 'I have got a great affection for Ireland. I really think it is a remarkable – it is a sort of magical country where almost anything could happen. You set your foot on Irish soil, you feel you're back in 1912 or something like that, and that suits me very well.' D.G. Duerden: 'Profile of Carel Weight' *Arts Review* 3 April 1965

*As I wend to the shores . . .* was, however, painted before Weight's first visit to Ireland.
He spoke briefly to me about Jack Yeats. 'He did much that was wonderful, but so many pictures are indifferent it's hard to understand why he troubled to paint them.'

5 Now in the Prado, Madrid.
6 Rosenthal conversation. Op. cit.
7 Wordsworth: 'Lines Composed a Few Miles above Tintern Abbey' *Lyrical Ballads* 1798.
8 Levy: op. cit.
9 Ibid.
10 Ibid.
11 In his article on *The Griselda Story*, Dr Robin Kirkpatrick writes that

> the theme is allied to the notion that the intellectual must free himself from the entanglements of married life if he is to have leisure and peace for contemplation.

> Robin Kirkpatrick: 'The Griselda Story in Boccaccio, Petrarch and Chaucer' *Chaucer and the Italian Trecento* (Cambridge University Press, 1983).

In the situation Carel Weight depicts, the nightwatchman is in the enviable position the intellectual has to struggle for. From his superior neutrality, the nightwatchman observes 'the disruptive power of love'.
12 Wordsworth: Preface to the *Lyrical Ballads* 1800–1802.
13 Browning: 'Childe Roland to the Dark Tower Came' *Men and Women* 1855.
A large water tower at the top of Campden Hill Road. An unprepossessing feature (now demolished), it filled a neurotic old lady living nearby with odd feelings of disquiet. 'It dominated her life,' said Carel Weight. 'I was fascinated with it myself. It was a tremendous landmark. Visible all over London.'

## 6 THROUGH THE SIXTIES I

1 Conversation with Norman Rosenthal in the catalogue of the RA Retrospective Exhibition, 1882. Op. cit.
2 The comment (in typescript) was attached to the manuscript of *The Curious Captain* in the Imperial War Museum. It did not appear in the published version of the book.
3 T.S. Eliot: 'The Dry Salvages V' *Four Quartets* (Faber, 1944).
4 Pope: *The Rape of the Lock*, Canto I.
5 Mervyn Levy: Introduction to the catalogue of Fieldborne Galleries' Exhibition, 1972. The remark is attributed to Carel's mother who – according to Carel Weight – was not present on the occasion.
6 President's Foreword to the catalogue of the Stanley Spencer Exhibition, Royal Academy of Arts, 1982.
7 Levy: op. cit.
8 Rosenthal conversation. Op. cit.
9 From W. Heywood's translation of *I Fioretti*, Chapter XXI. It appeared under the title *The Little Flowers of the Glorious Messer St Francis and of his Friars* (Methuen, 1906).
10 T.S. Eliot: *Four Quartets – East Coker*, I and II.
11 Mount Purgatory (in Dante's scheme) is encircled by two Terraces and Seven Cornices. By these stages the soul progresses to the summit, where it enters the Earthly Paradise and is prepared for its ascent to the Paradise of Heaven. The Seven Cornices are for the purgation of the Seven Deadly Sins.

## 7 THROUGH THE SIXTIES II

1 See the *Daily Telegraph* 27 January 1971.
2 Among the better known of Cruikshank's punning captions are:

> *The Night Ma(yo)re* (1816)
> *The Pursuit of Letters* (1828)
> *The Gin Juggernath, or The Worship of the Great Spirit of the Age!* (1834–6)
> *Quarter Day* (Comic Almanack, 1844)

See J.R. Harvey: *Victorian Novelists and their Illustrators* (Sidgwick and Jackson, 1970)
Catalogue of the George Cruikshank Touring Exhibition, Arts Council of Great Britain, 1974.
3 The stanza is from 'The Immortal Part' in *A Shropshire Lad*.
4 See Bede (672–735): *Ecclesiastical History* (c731).
5 Anatole France (1844–1924): *Le mannequin d'osier* Chapter XIX (1897).

## 8 A PORTFOLIO OF THE SEVENTIES

1 Proust: *A coté de chez Swann – Combray* (*A la recherche du temps perdu*) 1913–25.
2 See M.R. James: *The Apocryphal New Testament* (Oxford, 1924). From the Coptic text of Evodius.
3 See *The Times* 31 May 1972.
4 See *Les Contemplations*, Poem IX, Livre Quatrième (V. Hugo).
5 Bernard Sternfield held several exhibitions of Carel Weight's work in his gallery in St John's Wood (The Fieldborne Galleries). He wrote an appreciative and informative Introduction for his exhibition: *Carel Weight: Seven Decades* (1989). It included work as early as the 1929 portrait of his father and as recent as *The Strange Woman* (1989).
6 See A.E. Housman: *A Shropshire Lad* (1896) Poem XXVII.
7 A corrective is necessary here. Munch, in early life, was drawn to the Bohemian Movement in Christiania (Oslo), but could agree with few of their precepts. He rejected outright the second of these: 'Thou shalt sever thy family roots.' He was at one with his family in their tragic suffering, and was particularly devoted to his elder sister, Inger.
8 The phrase is from *Das Heilige – The Idea of the Holy* (1917) by Rudolf Otto (1869–1937), the German theologian, philosopher and historian of religion.
9 From Joseph Conrad: *The Mirror of the Sea* (Methuen, 1906).

## 9 WEATHERS AND OTHER SUBJECTS – THE LATER STYLE

1 From *Gerontion* by T.S. Eliot (*Poems*, 1920).
2 The scene is outside Wandsworth Station – 'a rather

depressed, run-down area.' (C.W.)

The landscape context mirrors and extends the emotions of his characters. In a mysterious way, the trees, skies, and even the stones of the dingy streets, take upon themselves the burden of human fear and loneliness. What, in human terms may seem trivial and incomprehensible suffering, becomes, through these landscapes, altogether grander, more profound.

Donald Hamilton Fraser: Introduction to the catalogue of the Carel Weight Exhibition, September 12–October 10, 1970 in the Reading Museum and Art Gallery

3 This cartoon appeared in *The Comic Almanack*, 1837.

4 The wide common = Wimbledon Common.

5 The subject of several prints. For instance: *Oiso – Rain on May 28* and *Tsuchiyama* (*The Fifty-Three Stations of the Tokaido*, 1834), and *The Kanda River from Shokei Bridge* (*One Hundred Famous Views of Edo*, 1856).

6 In *Paisaje de la Gran Roca* – etching and aquatint by Goya (c1800–1805).

7 The Two Inseparables are Francesca da Rimini and Paolo da Rimini in the 'Whirlwind of Lovers' (*Inferno*, Canto V).

8 The scene of the *Primavera* is outside Grantchester, Cambridgeshire.

9 James Thomson (1700–48): *The Seasons – Spring* (1728).

10 The owner of *The Seven Deadly Sins* writes, 'My instructions to Carel were: "Seven paintings, neither too big nor too small, having one dimension in common." '

Later, worrying over an appropriate arrangement for the panels, 'with scraps of paper on the kitchen table' as templates, he found the square format of *Lust* occupied inevitably the pivotal position at the junction of transom and vertical. The other square panel, *Pride*, lodged firmly at the base, the solid, concluding period to the cross.

No discussion had taken place between the artist and his patron concerning these minute particulars. It was, according to the patron, 'a perfect example of serendipity.'

11 See Carel Weight: 'The Training of a Painter III – Stimulation and Development of Imaginative Powers' *The Artist* May 1956.

12 The Anglo-Saxon is:

*And ic synnum fáh,*
*forwunded mid wonnum. Geseah ic wuldres treow.*

## 10 GHOSTS, CURIOSITIES AND THE SUBSTANCE OF NIGHTMARE

1 Alexander Gilchrist: *The Life of William Blake* Chapter XXXVI (Macmillan, 1863).

2 Charlotte Brontë: Preface to *Wuthering Heights* (1850).

3 V.H. Collins: *Ghosts and Marvels* (Oxford, 1924).

4 Mervyn Levy: *Carel Weight*. Op. cit.

5 The famous short shift worn by the young Witch-Novice, Nanny, in Robert Burns' *Tam o' Shanter*.

6 A nice story attaches: Weight's opposite neighbour surprised him one morning:

A delightful woman with a great sense of fun. I didn't know her very well at the time, and she suddenly crossed the road and said, 'I've got a bone to pick with you!'

'I do hope it's not serious,' I said.

'Well – since you painted the picture of all those witches coming out of my house, it's knocked £10,000 off its value!'

It's very sad that she moved out of the district, because we became fast friends.

7 The illogic deepens the element of disquiet. A dramatic device practised by Stanley Spencer, especially in *Swan Upping* (1914–19) and *The Cookham Resurrection* (1923–6).

8 M.R. James in *Ghosts and Marvels*. Op. cit.

9 Keith Roberts in *The Burlington Magazine* May 1968.

10 Carel Weight in *The Royal Academy Magazine* No 4, 1984.

11 See Chapter I, page 16.

12 See the closing lines of *The Waggoner* by Edmund Blunden:

. . . in the dim court the ghost is gone
From the hug-secret yew to the penthouse wall
And stooping there seems to listen to
The waggoner leading the grey to stall,
As centuries past itself would do.

From *The Waggoner and Other Poems* (1920) Sidgwick and Jackson.

13 The quotation is from W.B. Yeats' 'The Circus Animals' Desertion' (*Last Poems*, 1936–9).

# Index

Numbers in *italic* indicate illustrations    n = notes